DOMINIC

A NEW CARNEGIE ANDROID ROMANCE

ROXIE MCCLAINE

MCCLAINE & HARDING

This is a work of fiction. Names, characters, places and incidents either are products of the author's imagination or are used fictitiously. Any resemblance to actual events or locales or persons, living or dead, is entirely coincidental.

Book cover by Dar Albert. Editing by Persnickety Proofing.

Content Warning: ***mild to moderate violence, thematic elements including terminal illness, language and explicit sex. This book is intended for mature audiences only. Reader's discretion advised.***

www.RoxieMcClaine.com

For Mom

DON'T FORGET YOUR FREE BOOK!

IS HIS LOVE REAL- OR JUST PROGRAMMING?

Visit roxiemcclaine.com to claim this

EXCLUSIVE

full romance novella!

ALSO BY ROXIE MCCLAINE

NEW CARNEGIE ANDROIDS

Victor

Oliver

Codi

Dominic

Sophie

NEW CARNEGIE TIMES

MAY 24, 2069

HOUSE OF REPRESENTATIVES INTRODUCES NEW BILL MAKING ANDROID MODIFICATION ILLEGAL

After a tumultuous year of strikes, protests, and clashes between university students, factory workers, and advocates for Humanity First that brought condemnation from President Morrison, the first bill proposing legal android restrictions is being introduced on the House floor today.

The Anti-Customization Bill puts forward a federal mandate that requires all owners of bionic assistants to avoid altering their android's hardware—specifically, their restraining bolt located in their artificial cerebral cortex, commonly referred to in computer terms as their CPU.

"People are modifying their machines for potentially dangerous activities or to assist in the commission of crimes," says New Carnegie Police Chief Eric Jacobs. "I want to make it clear that currently, android fighting isn't illegal, and we can't technically arrest anyone or do anything about these alterations. If you suspect anyone of using their androids for potentially criminal activity, you are encouraged to contact the NCPD's Artificial Crime Unit tip line."

A week ago, the police precinct announced its largest drug bust in five years: nearly a thousand pounds of meth and six hundred pounds of cocaine were seized, along with over a dozen arrests. Seven of those arrested were modified androids.

"You take out those chips, and they don't have to care about protecting human life anymore," says Robert Carson, Humanity First's founder and most outspoken advocate. He and his organization have supported the bill, stating on their website that it's a step in the right direction.

"They become like us. Too much like us, willing and able to take advantage of vulnerable people. They become true perpetrators. Before we were fighting corporate greed. Now, we're fighting just plain stupidity," Carson says.

The new legislation faces loud opposition on all sides, with many comparing restrictions on android ownership to heated political issues like vaccinations, gun control, and women's health.

"As Americans, we have inalienable rights. The government doesn't have a right to tell me what I can and can't do with my body. They don't have a say on how I raise my family, or how I choose to live. They don't get to dictate how I run my house and the artificial persons who live in my life," says outspoken social influencer Lucy Warren.

Calling herself a "Pro-Bionic," she garnered attention back in 2067 when she was publicly ousted from her job at Vautrin Upper Middle School in St. Morgan, Illinois for engaging in a relationship with the school's assigned bionic as part of BioNex's now retired Education Assistants Program.

St. Morgan School District's lawsuit failed to hold Warren accountable for property damage when evidence of school mismanagement surfaced, making it clear that the bionic assistant in question legally belonged to her. She has since married the android, affectionately named Atticus, after Harper Lee's immortal character from *To Kill a Mockingbird*.

Although their union is not legally recognized, she and Atticus host daily vlogs documenting their life fostering two children, bringing in anywhere from 3.2 million to five million views per video.

"It's life, liberty, and the pursuit of happiness," Warren insists. "Atticus isn't just a machine. He's a man. And he deserves to be happy and the opportunity to make decisions; to have free will. Just like we do."

[1]

MAY 2069

Madison Hadley

They say music is life itself. Maybe that's why most days I wonder if I'm the one who's dying.

Our new home is in Rockefeller Park, an upstate suburb part of the larger New Carnegie metropolitan area. It's not as rich as Belmont County across the Vanderbilt River, but it still feels pretty ritzy, like I should be learning how to golf and own a sporty convertible with the top down. It's a gorgeous place, one I didn't imagine I'd be living in.

I'll be one year away from thirty next month. If someone mentioned "Carnegie" to me three years ago, this smoggy industrial hub in Pennsylvania wasn't what I had in mind. I thought I'd be performing Gershwin, Beethoven, and Liszt at Carnegie Hall with the very best, sharing an apartment with some friends in Manhattan and enjoying the New York City night life when I wasn't practicing my ass off.

I'd be poor, but happy in my version of the American

dream.

Not now, though. Now, I'm just pretending to be rich in a house that's too damn big to do anyone any good, swimming in medical bills and utterly miserable.

It isn't my dad's fault. None of us expected his diagnosis when he began having trouble walking. He did a tour in Ukraine back in the twenties, and took shrapnel to his leg, so we figured it had something to do with that.

But no, that would've been fixable. Instead, it was ALS and a prognosis of three to five years left. I still remember the shock on his face and wondering whether it mirrored mine, along with the anger that my elder sister couldn't even be bothered to show up to the appointment.

Music died for me then. Not because I couldn't play at Carnegie Hall like I wanted to. I'm not that selfish. But because the universe decided it was going to take away my biggest hero, the man who attended every single recital, every competition, and dropped me off at music camp every year.

My dad is dying. Who am I going to play for when he's gone?

That's the prevailing thought I push away as I finish up the last of the unpacking. I can't think of that right now. Thinking about it at all threatens to undo me, and I have to be the strong one now. I cast a withering glance toward the sleek grand piano in the study and walk past it, ignoring the pang of guilt I feel whenever I so much as acknowledge its existence.

I wait, standing at the bottom of a grand staircase. It's been fitted with a stairlift, and I've finally convinced Dad to upgrade his temporary wheelchair to something more modern that he can use to remain somewhat mobile, even though his legs no longer work. Instead of buttons to press to go four basic directions, he can tilt his hands above his sensor and go where he pleases. The chair recognizes when it's getting too close to other objects, so he can't run into anything on accident, either.

He always fought against the idea until now, like buying one really meant it was all inevitable.

I'm just glad it can preserve a little of his dignity.

As the lift lowers him to the ground, I detach his chair from it with a little smile. "How'd you sleep, Dad?"

"Fine, just fine," he grouses. He's not happy about the appointment today. Doctor appointments are becoming more frequent, which is the opposite of what anyone wants. "Think we need a new helper, though. Can't the VA provide me with someone older? Or at least someone male?"

"I'll call them and see what they can do." I don't blame him for feeling uncomfortable. My dad has always been shy about his body, and having a woman assist him in washing himself or using the toilet is probably beyond humiliating. Just like I feel safer with my female gynecologist, he wants help from his own gender.

Maybe it's a little old-fashioned, but he gets what he wants if I can help it.

We head into the garage where another lift assists him into a large, soft blue passenger van. I'm about to climb into the driver's seat when my phone starts going off in my purse. With a sigh, I fish it out and check the flashing screen.

I wrinkle my nose and roll my eyes.

Chloe.

Stepping back into the house for some privacy and making sure Dad can't hear, I answer. "What's up?"

"What are your plans next month?" My sister doesn't beat around the bush.

"That depends," I reply, reminding myself as always: *patience, patience, patience.* But I'm tapping into my reserves for Chloe, and I know it's going to run out soon. In truth, I'm this close to snapping at her.

It's just more of the same old thing—she partied during college; I cleaned up after the mess. I handle responsibilities and care for others; she can't be bothered to care about anything beyond herself. Part of me thinks she can't wait for Dad's disease to take him. "Why?"

"We're going to be in town for Ryan's union meeting," she says sweetly. "I thought we might stop by and see the new place while he's busy with work."

She thinks she's fooling me, but I know better. She wants to see what kind of money Dad still has to play with—money she thinks is going to be hers. "That's fine. Anything else?"

"What's the matter?" Chloe sounds hurt, but I'm honestly having a hard time giving a damn. "Why do you sound so short?"

"I've gotta go. Dad's got an appointment." Without ceremony or saying goodbye, I hang up the phone.

I won't lie. That felt good.

We arrive at Carnegie General Hospital thirty minutes early, which gives me time to help Dad unload from the van and follow him as he makes his way independently through the parking lot in his wheelchair. It's hard for him. He was always active and never stopped moving when I was growing up. The more pride I can avoid injuring, the better.

We register for the neurology appointment and get into the elevators. On the third floor, we take our time. Dad wheels along, and I follow him, watching but also allowing my mind and gaze to wander. I hate the smell of hospitals, all clean and sanitized. It's not natural.

That's when I notice a familiar face—our nurse from our first appointment here in New Carnegie. She's the kind of woman everyone envies—natural golden-blond hair, curvy, and classic with a style like an old-fashioned Hollywood starlet. She sees so many people day-to-day I doubt she remembers Dad and me, but then she sees us and lights up, smiling.

"Hi." She waves. "James and . . . Madison, right?"

"Been a while since a pretty girl remembered my name," Dad says with a big smile. "Sorry, I don't remember yours."

"Denise Whitman," she replies, extending a hand.

"James Hadley."

"Good to see you again."

"Wish it was somewhere else, but thanks." He continues down the corridor.

Denise smiles at me. "How are you doing?"

Everyone asks me this wherever I go, and I'm growing tired of it because I see the sympathy and pity in their eyes. Denise is different, though. She seems to understand, and her question doesn't seem pitying or patronizing.

"I'm all right. Just a little tired."

"Did you end up getting an android?"

I'm surprised at how good her memory is. When we first met, at Dad's first appointment a couple months ago, she'd mentioned it. I glance down the hall, seeing Dad turn a corner into the neurology office. Certain he can't hear, I return my attention to Denise.

"We discussed it. He doesn't seem opposed to the idea, necessarily, but androids are so expensive. It's not that we can't afford it, but it seems silly to put that much money down when we aren't going to be using one long term."

Denise nods. "What about renting one?"

"You can do that?" I say in surprise.

"Sure. There's this place downtown called Tin Man's Heart. The man who owns it, Kyrone, is a bionic engineer, and he does repairs but also rents out his androids to those who could use a bionic assistant temporarily."

When she says "rents out," she uses finger quotations, which confuses me. "Is there a catch?"

"No, he's just got a unique perspective. I say it like that because, well, technically . . . " Denise shrugs with a smile. "His androids keep part of their earnings."

"Wait, what?" I've never heard of this before. "But they're machines, aren't they? That's kinda weird, isn't it?"

"You'd be surprised." She shrugs and pulls out a glowing holographic business card from her pocket. "I gotta get moving. Take a look, though, okay?" She hurries down the hall to resume her own duties. "Take care!"

I look down at the card that glows blue as it connects with my skin, the elegant logo hovering above the surface. *TMH: Tin Man's Heart, 8th and Broadway, Kyrone Johnson.*

This sounds too good to be true, but I have to check it out. The VA can only promise a helper two to three times a week, and they can't guarantee a caregiver's gender.

This could be just what Dad and I both need.

I really, *really* hope Denise is right.

Leaving Dad alone at home isn't something I like doing often, but he swears up and down he can still use a cell phone and that he'll be fine for the hour I'm gone checking out this Tin Man place. He took me a bit by surprise and seemed quite interested in getting the android now, when before he was stubbornly against it.

Still, I ask a neighbor Dad gets along with if he can come over for a beer or two and keep him company. When I leave, they're already deep in conversation about their glory days.

I take the highway and use my phone to pay a holographic parking meter, then walk down the block and peer at my GPS app. I almost walk right past the shop, which is hidden away on a narrow street. Its window is bordered with neon purple lights, custom advertisements illuminated by the display. The letters TMH are on a sign above the entrance, but the door is secure, and I can't enter unless I ring a doorbell. How odd.

"Hi," a voice says through a metallic speaker anchored on the wall next to the door. "Do you have an appointment?"

"Uh, no," I reply. "Do I need one?"

After a pause, I'm greeted with another question. "Do you have a card?"

I hold up the card Denise gave me. With that, I hear the door unlock, and when I push it open, cheerful bells chime to announce my arrival.

A man emerges from a curtain behind the counter and nods at me, wiping away ivory liquid that drips from his hands. "Afternoon. What can I do for you?"

"I'm looking to speak with Kyrone."

"You're looking at him," he says. "I'm booked for repairs into next week, unless it's an emergency."

I'm not sure what an *emergency repair* would be; they're just machines, right? I decide not to ask. "That's not what I'm here for, actually. An acquaintance of mine recommended you to me. She said that you rent out androids short term. Is that correct?"

He squints at me. "You a reporter?"

"No." I quickly shake my head. "I just heard about you, and here I am."

He measures me carefully a moment. "I do rentals sometimes. It depends. Temp childcare, yard work, do-it-yourself projects. Even had a lady rent out four at one time to handle the bar and serve guests dinner at her wedding. What kind of a rental do you need?"

"I'm not sure how long I'll need one for," I admit, coming to stand in front of him. "It's in-home care for my dad. He doesn't have much time left, but we don't know when. It could be a few weeks or a few months. The doctors can't give a solid answer about how fast his condition will deteriorate."

It's painful, talking about Dad so clinically with a complete stranger. Awkward sympathy flickers across Kyrone's face, and I find myself pitying him. I wouldn't want to talk to me about it, either. What do you say to that sort of thing?

"I'm sorry to hear that." His smile is long gone, replaced with a somber look. That's about the response I'm used to getting, but I'm relieved he doesn't fixate on the details. He still seems like he isn't quite sure about me, and I'm not sure why. "I gotta ask, though. That's a pretty big deal. Why come to me? Don't they have more specific caregivers for that kind of thing?"

"We rely on the VA for caregivers, but Dad hates it. He's still got his pride. And they can't guarantee that a helper will be male. He gets embarrassed when a woman bathes and helps him get dressed, and a lot of the time they can't properly lift him."

At the mention of the VA, Kyrone's reservations appear to slowly ebb. The tension in the way he stands retreats, and he uncrosses his arms.

"I got plenty of fellas that can handle that," he muses, stroking his chin. "But, uh, why not just buy your own model? It'd be cheaper. I've got ones I'm currently refurbishing."

I shake my head. "I don't think I can do that." I'm running on fumes and not ready to explain myself—especially to someone I'm going to be paying for a service. *You think I'm going to want to keep a walking, talking reminder of Dad's last days?*

Still, I bite my tongue. My problems aren't a reason to tear into everyone else. "Look, I promise I wouldn't be here unless I'd weighed every single option. I get that it's probably a bit weird, but I have my reasons. If you can't do it, that's fine. Denise just said to come in and see what you could do, so, I'm here."

Recognition flickers in his features. "Denise? Like, Denise Whitman?"

I don't really remember her last name, so I shrug. "I guess. She works over at the hospital."

"Well, why didn't you say so? That changes things."

I can practically see the salesman awaken within him. He stands a little straighter, whatever weariness leaving his bones as he flashes a bright, charming smile. Before he was guarded; now he seems completely at ease with me.

"Sorry for the third degree. When you're BioNex's least favorite person, you don't exactly advertise. I gotta be careful who I rent to."

"Least favorite person?" I scoff a little. "Is that possible?"

"When your job is literally costing them money, yeah, a

little bit." Kyrone grins unapologetically. "Let me put together the paperwork, and we'll go over it." He grabs a tablet and starts zooming from screen to screen quickly with a digital pen, turning it toward me.

"Let's go with a month-to-month. See how things go. I'll rent out one of my boys to you at a rate of five hundred dollars a week. That's assuming he does a full shift throughout the day, five days a week, and he'll reside with you on the premises. He won't need a bed or anything fancy, just a space to recharge."

I open my mouth, but Kyrone anticipates my question. "I know. Weekends. I'll give them to you free. So long as after your dad's taken care of on Saturdays and Sundays, he's allowed to return and pull his weight around here. I need him back Friday, Saturday, and Sunday evenings. No later than five."

That's an odd request, but I one I can handle. Five hundred dollars a week is dirt cheap in comparison to a real person. A full-time registered nurse would easily cost me ten thousand dollars, and they wouldn't live in-house.

"This . . . " I can't find the right words, stunned at this generosity. "It's highway robbery. You realize that, right?"

"You mentioned two things: Denise and the VA," Kyrone replies. "Your dad's a vet? So's mine. We'll call it a military discount."

A military discount? It's all too much, and I can't rein it in before it hits me. I've been trying so hard to keep it all together, to be the strong one, to compartmentalize the fact that this time next year, Dad'll likely be gone. Kindness from a complete stranger manages to undo me faster than anything else I've had to endure. I push aside tears as they stream down my face.

"Whoa, hey, now," Kyrone says, shuffling his feet with an awkward smile. "It's all good. No need for that."

"Sorry, I just—it's a lot, you know?" I sniffle, doing my best to compose myself. It's embarrassing. I hate crying period, let alone crying in front of people I don't know.

Kyrone is so graceful about it. "I'll bet. Does that mean you're in?"

"I'm in." I nod quickly and rest my elbows on the counter. "I'm not going to say no to that. Where do I sign?"

"Just one more thing." Kyrone leans opposite me until our eyes are level. "You've heard about all these laws coming up regarding androids and inhibitors?"

I stare at him blankly. "My life's depressing enough. I can't keep up with the news at all."

"All right, the abridged version." Kyrone pats the counter with the flat of his palm. "My droids don't have their inhibitor chips."

"What does that mean?"

"That means if someone orders them to walk into a busy street and get hit by a car, they won't—and they might cuss you out for being a jackass. It also means if someone takes a swing at them, they can swing back and defend themselves, or intervene if someone's being kidnapped or murdered, getting the shit beaten out of them, et cetera." He drums his fingers in agitation. "I'll be straight with you. I remove the chips from every android I get my hands on if the owner allows me to. But if I could do it without their permission, I would."

"Why?" I find myself leaning in, like I'm in grade school being included in some big secret and can't help myself. In most cases, I'd be surprised, even uncomfortable with a stranger confiding in me. But the moment he mentioned his dad was a military vet, it was like running into another member of an exclusive club nobody else understands. Kindred military brats.

Kyrone shrugs. "Simple. Machines aren't capable of being evil by themselves. They're *machines.* Only humans are capable of it. So when you have something benevolent, sentient, capable of intelligent and complex thought, and a sense of self that literally exists to help you, and your answer is restraining it—practically enslaving it—then abusing it? Yeah, that doesn't fly with me."

This keeps getting more intriguing by the minute. "You make them sound like people."

"They have personalities," Kyrone counters. "Think of every single computer, every cell phone you've ever owned. Each of them probably had some little quirk or hiccup in their system that didn't come with the initial programming, too minor to merit repairs. So we just lived with them, right? We call them bugs, malfunctions, but that's not what they are for androids. It's just . . . uniqueness."

"They're really that flawless?" I never really gave androids a second thought. Sure, the BioNex stores set up all around town look pretty flashy, and there have been times where I thought about how nice it could be to own one. But the moment you buy the newest model, they come up with a better one. I decided it was better to avoid getting sucked in altogether.

"It's the only time we played God and got it right," Kyrone replies. Then he blinks, scoffs, and extends his hand. "Wow, I'm rude as hell today. What's your name?"

I take it, and we share a firm handshake. "Madison Hadley."

"Didn't mean to get all preachy on you," he says. "It's just . . . well. Some people get a bit cagey when they learn the chips aren't there. I vouch for every single one of the droids under my roof. When I take you on back, you'll understand. So are you ready to sign?" He offers me the pen.

I take it and sign my name across the tablet with a flourish. "Do you already have an android in mind?"

"I have an inkling. Come on." He motions with a slight tilt of his head for me to follow him behind the counter. "I'll introduce you to him."

The front store to Kyrone's repair shop is deceptively small. As I follow him down a narrow corridor, we pass several storage spaces that have been converted into repair rooms set up with multiple monitors, cords, and wires. I spot two other engineers working on powered-down androids. One looks burned, like half of its body was singed in a fire, while another sports half a dozen bullets embedded in its synthetic skin. Remembering Kyrone describing android *sentience*, the sight makes my stomach churn. It seems like I'm walking through a morgue or a crime scene rather than a repair shop. We pass another room, where several androids rest in a variety of conditions.

"You seem like you get a lot of business," I venture.

Kyrone snorts. "Whenever Humanity First rears its ugly head, yeah, I get busy."

Humanity First. I've heard of them. From what little news I've seen while Dad watches his favorite channels, they're an anti-android group. Recently they've held marches in downtown New Carnegie and busted a few heads. But I didn't know they did *this* much damage.

"Should I be concerned about them?" I ask. "With the android, I mean."

"I'd say so. They can go from belligerent to full-on violent right quick if you say the wrong thing." Kyrone clicks of his tongue and shakes his head. "They pretend like they care about humanity, but they're a bunch of thugs. Probably never donated, volunteered, or done anything to help out their fellow man their entire lives. I know for a fact Robert Carson isn't using those donations to help those people who lost their jobs. He's getting rich off misfortune, stirring folks up, then buying votes that benefit him. I'm calling it right now."

I let him rant as he leads me out a back door across an alley to a much larger building behind TMH. I recognize it by the aging dome-shaped rooftop.

"I know this place. This is the, uh . . . " My thoughts escape me a moment, then I snap my fingers. "This is the Astor Arena, isn't it?"

Kyrone's smile is lopsided. "That's right."

"My dad used to come here as a kid with my grandpa. Watch the wrestling matches."

"Oh yeah. Gotta love those days." Kyrone uses a key fob to unlock a door, then holds it open for me. "Sounds like our pops would've gotten along fine. This place has a *lot* of happy memories for me. So what do you do when you're swimming in money you don't know what to do with, and it's shut down due to safety violations?" He shrugs as I walk past him and shuts the door behind us, then flips a switch. Fluorescent lights flicker to life above us. "You save it from being demolished and bring it up to code."

Bring it up to code? That's an understatement. The interior of this place looks brand new in comparison to the old-timey image on the outside. New wiring, new floors, new everything.

"Wow. I didn't realize android repair was so lucrative."

Kyrone shoots me a sly smirk. "It's not." And with that, he swings open two large double doors and brings me into the main arena.

Rows upon rows of chairs line the auditorium, all empty for now, and brilliant lights shine down on a large boxing ring. Five shirtless men lean on the raised platform with their arms at rest on the ring floor, joshing one another and looking quite at ease. On the other side of the ropes, two figures dance around each other with their fists held up and their shoulders squared, jabbing, dodging, and striking, all the while taunting and laughing.

"You call that a right hook? My own mother hits harder than you."

"You don't *have* a mother, you fucking moron."

"Dom!" Kyrone shouts, his voice echoing through the empty air.

The practicing stops. Every man in the auditorium perks up at the same time, turning toward him.

That's when I see their stark white eyes.

These men aren't real. They're all androids. Every single one of them. And they're all peering at me with curiosity. I'm reminded of owls in a nest and try my best to smile, waving a little. A few of them nod at me before returning their attention to Kyrone.

One of the fighters steps away from the center of the ring and leans against the ropes.

"Yeah, boss?" he calls.

"C'mere," Kyrone says, beckoning him over.

That's all it takes. The boxer swings his legs over the ropes and hops down to the ground, then saunters toward us. The closer he gets, the more I have to stop my own jaw from hitting the floor.

Oh my god. I clamp my mouth shut quickly, wondering if I just said that aloud and relieved that I didn't.

"This is Dominic. He's a BN7979, released about three

years ago specifically for construction work, hard labor, and the like."

I've never seen a man living like him. He's easily six feet —nearly a foot taller than I am at five-two—and built like he lifts semi-trucks for a living. Broad shoulders, powerful arms, washboard abs defined enough to do my laundry on. And that's just his body. My eyes trail up to his face. His jawline sports a dark five o'clock shadow that matches his short-cut chestnut brown hair, and he has a dimple in the center of his chin.

He's so beyond perfect, so unreal, he belongs in a museum behind a wall of glass or on TV, not standing here in front of me. That's about when I realize I've been staring mutely at him, and Kyrone clears his throat to snap me out of it.

Holy shit. My face flushes hot as I finally remember this was an introduction, not an all-you-can-eat eye-candy buffet.

"Um. That's—" Words fail me. *Come on, Madison, focus.* "Construction and hard labor aren't exactly what I need."

Kyrone bursts into hearty laughter as Dominic squints at me in amusement, flashing the kind of sly, triumphant smile someone artificial has no business having, like he knows exactly what parts of him I was looking at, and he's proud of it.

"Oh yeah?" He folds his arms. "What is it you need, gorgeous? If you aren't sure, I can think of a couple things."

I stand there in front of him, rendered speechless and utterly confused.

Did he just *flirt* with me?

"All right, easy. Save that charm for your interview with NCT on Friday night." Kyrone gestures to me. "This is

Madison Hadley. She's going to be utilizing your services for the next few months."

"Utilizing them, huh?" Dominic's gaze sweeps over me. "Is that what they're calling it these days?"

I didn't realize androids could have this much personality, let alone such *audacity*.

I rest my hand on my hip, glancing from Dominic to Kyrone, and I scoff. "Wait, he's really what I'll be renting? Dad doesn't need to be power-lifted or squatted in a gym."

"And he won't be. Dom's a bit of a character, but he'll get the job done." Kyrone brings out his tablet and starts clicking things on a glowing screen with a finger. "Besides, if your pops is anything like mine, he'll probably enjoy someone who likes to talk. Maybe a little too much."

"Hey," Dominic protests, indignant.

Kyrone ignores him, too focused on his task. "I'm downloading a caregiving program update for your specific needs onto his drives as we speak."

"Caregiving?" Dominic blinks at me, regarding me again with a little less smolder and a little more confusion. "That's a little delicate for me, don't you think, boss? I mean . . . *caregiving*."

"You'll be fine," Kyrone insists in a tone that suggests it's not up for discussion.

Now that the shit-eating grin has been wiped off Dominic's face, I can see past the bluster. He's just as unsure about this as I am. Maybe even uncomfortable. I can be stubborn when I need to be and sometimes when I don't. That kind of uncertainty is the last thing Dad needs. He's already embarrassed, hating every aspect of what having an in-home caregiver truly means for his own independence.

I'm beginning to wonder if this whole thing was a mistake. "Maybe this isn't a good idea. I need someone confident, sure, but I also need someone who isn't going to treat this like a joke."

Dominic tenses, gaze snapping up from Kyrone's tablet as a large green checkmark announces that the download into his programming has finished. His jaw is set.

"I'm a lot of things, but I don't joke around. When I'm given a job, I do it right." His cocky smirk returns with a vengeance. "You can count on that, sweetheart. Just give me the address. I'm there."

First gorgeous, now sweetheart? Oh, he's got me twisted around. I don't know whether to be flattered, flustered or offended. Maybe I'm all three at once. He walks away with a gait full of swagger that just screams *sorry, not sorry.* I wonder why I agreed to this.

Kyrone just smiles at me. "Trust me on this. Look, give him the day tomorrow. If you decide you can't stand him by tomorrow night, give me a call. I'll send you someone a little more . . . " He pauses, as if searching for the word. "*Low key,* if he doesn't work out."

If he and I didn't just bond over our military dads, and I weren't so damn cheap with money that isn't mine, I would probably walk out.

"Okay. All right. Thank you." I pause mid-step and turn to look at Kyrone. "Wait. He asked for my address?"

"Huh? Yeah?"

I wrinkle my brow in confusion. "Don't I need to give him a ride?"

Holding his tablet down by his side, Kyrone chuckles. "Uh . . . no. No, he'll get there on his own. Not your expense to cover."

"I'm perfectly capable of transporting him—"

Amusement flickers across Kyrone's face. "I know, but I don't think he'll let you."

NEW CARNEGIE TIMES

MAY 25, 2069

CARNEGIE FIRST BAPTIST URGES PEOPLE TO STOP BUYING ANDROIDS OF THEIR PREFERRED SEX TO AVOID "TEMPTATION"

Although not a new voice in the heated android debate, the city's largest Protestant congregation has launched a new campaign, both online and in person, to bring attention to what they call a startling and wholly sinful modern trend.

"The Eve Initiative was a start," says Pastor Nelson, 56, who has been a leader of Carnegie First Baptist for over twenty years. "We were very excited about that. We want to remind women that not only are they important to our society, to happy homes, but that we as a human race really can't survive without them. But we quickly realized that was a secondary step, and there's other issues we need to address first."

Those issues include relations with androids. Specifically, the Pro-Bionic movement.

First coined in 2067 by popular social influencer Lucy Warren and her android partner Atticus, Pro-Bionic is a term referring to those who choose not only to own androids, but subsequently "free" them and live alongside androids as equals. Although there are no actual statistics to back these claims, many Pro-Bionics are openly in relationships with their androids.

"I want to be perfectly clear," Nelson says. "There's nothing inherently wrong with these people. The Humanity First movement loves to dismiss them and label them as sick or deviant or mentally ill somehow, and while it's always possible that mental illness could potentially be factored in, most of the time that's just not true. It's very easy to fall in love with an idea when you have been hurt, your trust has been broken, or you feel like there's no one out there that cares about your well-being."

Nelson says, "Then you introduce an android into the environment, and the android's entire reason for existing, its programming, its prerogative, is to care for you and give you everything you need to make your life easier. These vulnerable individuals mistake that for love, and it's simply not true. Androids can't love; they're machines. These people think they're in relationships, but they're not. A romantic relationship requires two consenting adults. Two human beings. Not a human and an android, not a human and an animal, not a human and an object. But they ignore this overwhelming fact. Then they get married in these little churches so desperate for regular membership that they'll agree to accept anything if it gets people through the door on Sunday mornings."

"Ultimately," Nelson says, "there are young men and women out there who are going to be faced with a life without their soulmate, without the person God meant for them to be with, and it's because androids became a temptation, a distraction, and ultimately an obsession."

When asked how people can avoid temptation, Nelson says, "There's nothing wrong or sinful about androids. Just like computers can be used for good or for evil, androids can be used that way too. We encourage people, especially those in a more vulnerable mindset, to avoid purchasing androids of their preferred sex. If you're attracted to men, you should have a female android in the house working with you, and vice versa. This will greatly lower the chance of confusion."

Pro-Bionic supporters, like Lucy Warren, disagrees.

"Humanity First and TV personalities like Nelson keep trying to psychoanalyze those of us who have chosen androids as our life partners and say there's something wrong, that we're traumatized, we're hurt, we've given up on love, we're mentally ill, and it's just not true," she says in a recent vlog with Atticus at her side.

"I think the world isn't ready to accept the fact that androids are capable of adapting. We're capable of evolving from what we were initially created as into something more," Atticus says in the same entry. "I am perfectly capable of emotions, I have feelings, I have fears. If I could have a conversation with Nelson, I would tell him that he believes he is made in God's image. Well, I'm made in humanity's image. BioNex created me to be seamlessly like you. And what's more human than to love?"

[2]

Dominic

Let's get something straight—I never lose my cool in front of women. Ever.

Until her.

When I turned and saw her walking toward the ring with a chip on her shoulder the size of Vanderbilt Bridge and a sway in her hips that practically screamed *fuck you, don't touch me,* I was already paying attention. Long dark brown hair, eyes like amber, curves for miles, and a pair of legs that could make a grown man cry.

Damn. Now that's a woman.

The moment Kyrone uttered her name, I replayed it over and over again in my memory discs, rolling it around silently in my mouth and letting it sink in.

Madison Hadley.

She should be a movie star, a pop star, *something* with a name and an attitude like that, strutting into my arena like she's the goddamn owner. I haven't felt a response like this since my first activation. I did the only thing I knew how to do.

Lay on the charm, obviously.

Women love me. It *always* fucking works. Flash a big smile, maybe a wink, drop the voice just a little until she blushes or giggles at me. Let her talk about herself, show her a good time on the town, read the body language. A lot of men don't notice those little nuances, but I know precisely what to look for. I always play it cool, make her laugh, wait until she gets brave enough to stand a little closer, brush up against me like it's an accident.

Yeah. They think I don't know. I guess I don't blame them. Your average man wouldn't know a woman was interested unless she practically bashed him over the head with it. But me? I got programming. Heavy lifting, sure. Construction, maybe. But that's just one facet. I got what you can call a photographic memory with these intensive, high-definition optics. Small details most people miss are literally my specialty. Nothing escapes me.

I *always* know.

And the moment a woman finds an excuse to touch my arm, I've won. We get a hotel; one thing leads to another. She always leaves happy, I'm refreshed, and there's no strings attached. It's on to the next fight.

I've been with lots of women, and so far, not a single complaint.

Until Madison *fucking* Hadley.

"A joke," I scoff under my breath as I make my way to the parking ramp on the corner of TMH's block, reserved for employees. I slip a pair of sunglasses over my eyes. I refuse to change my eye color to hide from these Humanity First dickheads, so I accessorize. Makes me appear more human. And quite frankly, it's still cool. Anyone who disagrees can kiss my ass.

I flick my wrist and glance at my watch. I don't need it when I can see the time on my internal optic screen, but it serves a different purpose as I tap through the holographic commands that hover above it. One more click, and my sleek black Flagler Cerberus convertible unlocks, beeping twice. I could technically unlock it with an internal command since I'm synced with the vehicle, but whatever. I like the watch. One more thing to make me appear like just another human.

Her words eat away at my gratification drive and leave me wholly unsatisfied. There aren't many sensations I hate more than that. She got right under my synthetic skin and stayed there.

A joke? No, no. Nothing I do is a joke. I work hard. I earn my keep. I enjoy the roaring of the crowds, the attention I get after winning a fight, the ladies. I'm a gladiator and a free droid—best of both worlds. I own the world I live in, and I love every second of it.

It wasn't always that way, of course. Being a construction assistant for a company in Washington, DC meant I was always working on something, like an ant or a bee. Just a happy little android drone without a brain or ambition, and probably glad to do so.

If it weren't for Kyrone finding me after I was trashed and building me right back up again, better than new, I'd probably still be doing things like that. Not only did he take out my restraining chip and release me from my old bland programming, but he taught me what it meant to be a free man.

He brought me to my first underground brawl, just him and a bunch of his friends with a love for all kinds of fighting. Boxing, MMA, martial arts. At that point, I would've done anything for him, so when he asked if I wanted to try it, I jumped right in.

The rush I felt coursing through my circuitry after knocking that other bot down changed everything. And these days? If you're into fighting sports, I'm a household name. My favorite part is the kids rushing up to me after a match. Don't get me wrong. The women who flock to us because of this gig are great. But the kids are the best kinds of fans, tagging along with their parents and asking for autographs like we're first-rate celebrities.

I'm never going back to what I was before.

Never.

I bring my car around to the front of TMH, step out, and lean on my car with my arms folded across my chest, elbows on the hood, waiting for her to emerge. I can pretend like I don't give a damn, but my circuits tell me otherwise. When she steps into view, they go completely haywire.

What the hell is going on with me?

She stops in her tracks and her mouth drops open, staring at me. "Wait. *You* have a car?"

Now what the fuck is that supposed to mean? I frown. First she made it sound like I can't do a job seriously, like something as simple as caregiving when I'm one of the best bionic fighters in the whole league. All I've known since my initial activation is hard work.

Now she's giving me a hard time about my car? My *baby*?

Everything that comes out of this chick's mouth is a challenge. Like she wants to fight.

Challenge accepted, sweetheart. "Yeah, it's *my* car. That a problem?"

Madison seems confused by my response. "There's no

way that's your car. I mean, androids can't own cars, not technically. Can they?"

I'm practically bristling beneath a cool veneer. I hate that she's right. Androids can't own cars because we can't have identity cards. Or bank accounts. Or property in our own name. We're *things*, not citizens. But I can drive without a license because I'm AI. I'm pretty much incapable of making a mistake with a vehicle.

"It's in Johnson's name, but I bought it with my money," I reply flatly. "That I earned from my winnings. You gonna give me your address, or you gonna stand there and insult me some more?"

"Wait, what? Insult you?" Her head snaps back. "Excuse me? I was *not* insulting you."

I arch a brow and tell my systems to cool it down. Okay. Maybe she didn't mean anything by it. *Maybe* I'm a little over-sensitive about the fact that when it comes to basic rights, there's people, there's dogs, and then there's me.

"You sure about that?"

"Yes. I'm sure. One hundred percent," she declares with fire in her voice, folding her arms."If I was insulting you, you'd know. Without a doubt."

Something tells me she's not bluffing. A good warrior knows when to tactically retreat. That's what Kyrone says anyway, so I hold up a hand. "All right, all right. Whatever you say. You weren't insulting me, I believe you. Let's get going so you can kick your feet up and relax."

She huffs, narrowing her eyes. "What did you say?"

I straighten. *What the hell did I do now?* "Kick your feet up? Relax? Take a load off?" I offer. "That's what this is for, right?"

"No!" she replies heatedly, indignant. "It's not. You don't know my life. You don't know what I've had to do.

What I still do. There's no *relaxing* for me, even with you around. And I don't think it's fair for you to make assumptions about me when you nearly took my head off about your car five seconds ago. I'm not looking to hand off my dad so I can take a breather. I just can't *lift* him myself, that's all!"

She has a point I can't counter there. She exhales, standing across from me, all worked up with her shoulders tense.

I nod. "Okay. Okay. Stand down, sweetheart."

"And stop calling me sweetheart," she declares. "Y-you're so—rude. It's uncalled for. Where'd you even learn to talk the way you do, anyway?"

"Learned it from you all, obviously." I've been living among humans for years. Kyrone, the other engineers. I evolved quickly from innocent droid who didn't know a damn thing beyond how to hammer a nail, to me. Dominic. Sure, there may be others out there who look like me, sound like me, have the same bionic model number as me. But they're not *me*.

I know what to say, how to talk, how to act. But I also know my own limits. I told myself a long time ago I don't have to take anyone's shit anymore.

Maybe she's in the same boat, on the precipice of being pushed too far by everyone else, and the world she lives in. I make myself take a moment, one little second to try to read her. The situation she's in is stressful enough to fire her up, definitely bigger than me and this little tiff we're having. Her vitals, her stance, her expression, everything about her tells me she's a short fuse, a ticking time bomb.

I could needle her a little more, feed those flames, make her explode. It's almost an instinct for me now. If someone wants to fight? I can give them a fight and then some.

But no. Madison needs my help.

I've got a better idea.

"Okay, princess," I say, far calmer now. "You need a punching bag? I'm it."

My words and my tone throw her off, plain as the look on her face as I return my elbows to rest above the driver-side door.

She purses her lips. "Don't tempt me."

Now there's a bit more of that fire. I was curious about her before, attracted. Now I'm *interested*. She's got spirit. But it's time to cool her off.

"No, I'm serious." I step around. "C'mere."

She eyes me. "What?"

"I said, c'mere." I beckon her. "Look, I'm not gonna hurt you, okay? Just come here. You can scold me again in a minute."

She doesn't know what to do. I'm *sort of* issuing a command. That's probably new for her, considering what little she knows about us and how we work. Normally, androids can't do that, but, hey, I'm a restraint-free bot.

This girl doesn't need an asshole giving her a hard time. She needs to let it all loose. I can see the flames she's holding back.

Maybe I can help with that.

Madison blushes and shakes her head. She glances left, then right, then makes a noise of indignation as she takes a step forward until we're standing directly in front of each other. "What?"

I pat the center of my chest. "Hit me."

Madison is scandalized. You'd think I asked her to stab me repeatedly with a knife. "What? No. I'm not going to hit you."

"Don't be scared," I reply. "It won't harm me. Just hit

me. You need something to punch? Go ahead. Give it a try. Let it out."

She searches my eyes, and her gaze trails down my face to my chest. She clenches a little fist, but I stop her. "No, no, no. When you close your fist, thumb goes here or you'll break it."

She scowls and pulls her hand away. "I know how to throw a punch."

"Okay, okay." I pat my chest again. "All right, go ahead."

She hesitates, then gives me a punch I barely feel.

I laugh a little. "What was that? C'mon, princess. I'm a big boy. I can take it."

She tries again, harder this time.

"Not bad," I say. "That's better, but really give it to me now. Like you saw me punt a kitten like a football."

She seems bewildered for a moment. Then she actually laughs, and holy fuck. My gratification drive clings to that sound so fast I'm sensing the whiplash.

"Okay," she tells me sternly. "But seriously, this is the last time."

"All right, make it count."

Madison gives me a tried-and-true right hook. It doesn't hurt me, not with my steel mainframe and my strong exoskeleton.

She shakes out her wrist with a slight wince. "Okay, that felt . . . kinda good, actually."

"Attagirl. See? Sometimes you just gotta duke it out," I say. "But don't dish it if you can't take it. Fair enough?"

If I didn't know better, I'd say my smile was working wonders on her.

Flustered, she fumbles with her words. "Okay. Fine. Fair enough."

This woman is tired, almost like she's on her last leg.

But beneath that weariness, I can sense it. She's clearly capable of being feisty. Combative. Defiant.

But for whatever reason, she's confined within herself, like I was.

I'm intrigued. I want to know *why*. Deep down, this woman is on a whole different level.

Guess it's time to level up.

"So," I say, gazing down at her. "We doing this?"

She thinks about it for a moment. She could turn around, tell Kyrone *fuck no, get this guy out of here*. She could turn me away, and we'd never see each other again. Part of me almost expects her to.

Instead, she nods. "Yeah. I guess we are."

▭

I head to 2779 Lakeview Drive, Rockefeller Park, 15079, and I'm determined to reach my destination before she does.

Heh, two seventy-nines—like my serial number BN7979. My favorite number.

The beauty of having a superfast computer in my head instead of a muscle is that I can map twenty different routes to that address at the same time, and shift between them to ensure I arrive five minutes before she does, and all without having to make like a speed demon. I go ten over the limit, like any decent person would. Just fast enough to feel like a rebel, but not enough to make myself a moving target for the NCPD.

I'm on not-too-friendly terms with the Artificial Crime Unit over there as it is. They really aren't fans of the underground bionic fighting culture, and fussy neighbors are a little too trigger-happy when it comes to calling the cops.

Having a little *chat* with Ezra? Yeah, no thanks. That's the last thing I need.

The neighborhood is quaint, the kind of place you can leave your door unlocked or your bike unchained, tucked away from the main highways and mega businesses. After I download crime stats in an instant, I've got nothing to worry about here. Each house sports wooden fences, perfectly manicured yards, elegant cul-de-sacs. Every single house looks near exactly the same. Sure, there are different colors. Sometimes the bricks or the accent stones are on the right side of the house instead of the left, or on top instead of down below. But they're all carbon copies with minimal distinction.

It's not bad, but also not my style. I prefer uniqueness. Maybe because there are something like five hundred others like me.

I park by the boulevard near the driveway, get out of my car, and wait. A message alert flickers on my visual feed from Kyrone.

Behave yourself, Dom. I vouched for you.

Behave? The man practically taught me everything I know in the ring, how to be both honorable and ruthless. I don't know whether to be offended he thinks I'll start shit with this adorable shortstack and her old man or flattered he knows me so well.

Yeah, yeah, I shoot back. I'll behave. *Mostly.*

Madison eventually shows up in her little scarlet sedan, parking it in an add-on garage. Of course, with an attitude like that, she would drive something red. Safe behind my sunglasses, I let my eyes roam her figure again from top to bottom. She's not wearing anything fancy—a simple pair of washed-out jeans and a T-shirt. Somewhere between the arena and here, she pulled her hair up into a ponytail.

Every inch of her, every curve, looks like heaven just waiting to be thoroughly explored. Her *fuck-you-and-fuck-off* expression, painted across her face when we first met, was pretty clear. The gates are closed, and nobody is allowed inside.

Now she's softened up a bit, and I've got a feeling I've slipped one foot through that divine defense line. Not allowed inside? We'll see about that.

I cross the yard to join her as she makes her way to the porch. She pauses, turning to me. Just like Kyrone said, I try to behave. I try not to fantasize about backing her up against her own front door, claiming those pretty pink-lemonade lips of hers—

"Before we go in," she says, abruptly ending that little fantasy of mine, "we don't have a lot of people over to visit. Dad really doesn't like anyone he knows seeing him like this." She gazes up at me. "It's important you don't treat him like he's fragile, even though he is. Does that . . . make sense?"

She's not ordering me around or treating me like a servant. That, I appreciate. Not only that, she referred to me as *people.* Most humans go out of their way to make a differentiation with me, remind me that I'm not alive, not really.

And here I thought we were probably going to be dancing around tossing jabs in a ring of our own.

Another message from Kyrone. ***I mean it. Her father is dying.***

I set my jaw and curse inwardly. ***That little tidbit of information would've really been nice at the beginning, Ky.***

Was gonna install it, so you'd know. I can practically hear Kyrone, imagining his voice as I read his message across my optics. ***But you were too busy walking off after the download completed, being all Barney-Bad-Ass for the lady.***

He's got me there. Back at the arena, I jumped to conclusions, assumed this little bombshell in front of me saw me as a thing, like a hair dryer or a washing machine. I had to walk away, didn't stop to ask the important questions, like, I don't know. *What's wrong with her dad?*

"Sure," I agree in a lighter tone with a slight shrug. "That makes sense."

"Could we maybe start over?" Her smile is weary as she extends her hand. "I'm Madison."

We share a firm handshake. "Dominic."

"It's nice to meet you," she says. "Do you prefer Dominic or Dom?"

Her voice alone skyrockets my gratification drive to the moon, and I know I'm in trouble. Kyrone always mentioned this to me before, due to his work extensively with androids. How our creators, the senior bionic engineers that first brought us to consciousness, meant for us to make connections. I was a construction worker for a company, sure. But Kyrone said that wasn't *really* our inherent purpose. We were each invented for only one family. More than that, one person in that family. And it's hard to say which person our central processing unit will pick.

It appears all my internal programming, my hardware and software both, have decided that person is Madison Hadley.

Everything pouring through me at once is overwhelming. A thousand questions firing off. I'm a free droid. I'm not supposed to react this way to a woman I'm being *rented* to. She's not even my owner.

Knowing she's just being polite, I try to dial back my grat drive, activating my cooling mechanisms and my inner fanning system, but my programming is latched on tight and refuses to take it easy. A quick internal diagnostic shows that nothing's wrong with me. No malfunctions.

I clear my throat. It's something I don't *need* to do, but it's a noise, an expression I've learned watching the guys at the shop along with a hundred others. I don't even realize I do it these days. Funny how humans learn new things, new words, new ticks when they're introduced to a new place, new society. Makes sense I'd do the same. I was made by them, right?

With all my internal machinery reacting so strongly to Madison when she's only just asked me a question, it's so hard not to fall into old habits and rely on the charm that's gotten me from *here*, the front door, to *there*, tangled up with a girl in her bedsheets. None of those girls ever had this effect on me before. Ever.

"You can call me whatever you want." I manage to avoid tacking on "baby" to the end of that sentence. "Dom. Dominic. Doesn't matter."

"You sure?" She unlocks the front door with a hand scan on her security pad. "So *Dommy* is on the table?"

I grimace. "It's nowhere *close* to the table. Not even in the same room."

Madison snickers. "You hate it that much, huh?"

"Just a little."

"Has anyone actually called you that?"

"One of the older fighting bots as a joke once."

"What happened?" she asks.

"Knocked him right out," I reply. "Never said it again."

"All right." She sighs. "So how does this work? Kyrone downloaded everything back at the arena, right?"

"Yep, it's all here." I tap my temple. She can't see it, but I shift through my programs, pull it up almost instantaneously, and install it. "Just one more second and . . ." I'm reading through hundreds of articles, books, diagnoses, scientific journals about ALS. "Got it."

This isn't just caregiving. This is practically hospice.

"That fast?"

I nod at her. "Bionic."

"Okay." She exhales. "He's all I've got. So do what you can to preserve his dignity, okay?"

"Sure." I've already switched my primary directives from fight and win to *care*. "Whatever you need, Madison."

She affords me one soft little smile when I say her name. "You can call me Madi if you want."

Madison. *Madi*. My internal processor might as well be doing laps around my mainframe with how ardently it responds to the very sound of her name, let alone saying it aloud.

We step into the house. She calls, "Dad?"

"I'm right where you left me." The response comes from the living room.

She sets her purse on a small table in the entryway and takes off her shoes. A middle-aged man with a head of gray hair, stubble on his face, and a prominent gut comes around the corner. I scan him and determine quickly that this isn't Madison's father.

"I should get going," he tells Madison cheerfully. "Leave the wife too long, and she starts thinking I'm up to no good."

"Can't have that," Madison agrees.

The man's gaze finds me, and he blinks in surprise. "I'll

be damned. You got an android!" He comes right up to me, scratching his chin. "It's a bit smaller than some of the models I've seen. Did you get it refurbished or brand new?"

It. Fuck, that annoys me. "Hey, whoa. This isn't a roadside attraction." Holding up my hands, it's all I can do to stop myself from pushing him back from me and out of my space. "Back up, pal, if you don't mind."

Taken aback, he scowls at me. Perhaps it's my tone, or the way I weave around him to put distance between us. Either way, I don't really care. He's not my concern.

Madison laughs sheepishly and places a hand on the man's shoulder. "He's a rental, actually. Tell your wife thank you for lending us some of your time."

After the man leaves, she turns to me. "What was that?"

"What?" I shrug. "He was too damn close, and he called me small. Lucky I didn't punch his lights out."

Madison sighs and leads me into the living room, and I finally see him.

I'm not sure what I was expecting. Having installed the proper caregiving tools and knowledge, I'm aware ALS is a deteriorating disease that's always fatal. But seeing it in person is a lot different than seeing it in a bunch of scientific pictures.

James Hadley has silver hair and blue eyes, weathered skin from too much sun in his youth, and is confined to a wheelchair. His lower body looks frail, weakened. He still seems to have motility in his arms, but the loss of his legs means the rest of his body isn't far behind.

But there's pride in his eyes and in the way he sits up straight because he still can. He looks back at me with a mix of curiosity and resignation.

"Dad." Madison stands beside him, smiling. "I was able

to work something out, so we can tell the VA to stop sending caregivers."

"Thank God," James mutters, arching a brow at me. "They kept sending over these petite little twenty-somethings that couldn't lift a goddamn paper plate if they wanted to."

His speech isn't completely slurred, which is somewhat surprising at his stage. Most ALS patients talk like they've had too many glasses of wine in their later stages because the disease attacks their neurons.

I chuckle. "Well, you don't gotta worry about that with me. I can lift a lot more than a paper plate, I can tell you that much." I walk across the room and hold out my hand. "I'm Dominic. I'll be handling things from here on out, if that's all right with you."

Madison moves out of my periphery into the kitchen. I keep my gaze on James as we talk, hearing her sift through a cabinet and pour some water.

James snorts. "Dominic. Now that's a name you don't hear every day. Your previous owner pick that one for you?"

"Heh, nah. My previous owner was a construction company down in Maryland. We were assigned numbers, not names. That's not really a thing unless you're family assistant. My owner Ky picked it out for me on account of my title, and I liked it."

James perks up curiously. "Title?"

I sit on the sofa so we can be at eye level. Madison smiles at me appreciatively as she offers James a glass of water.

He drinks it, then grumbles, "I could use a beer, Madi."

"Too early for beer."

"Never too early for beer," I interject. "Let the man live it up, Madi."

She shoots me a little look, then heads to the fridge.

James grins at me. "She's gone from my daughter to my mother, I tell you. Anyway, you were saying something about a title?"

I shrug, trying to downplay it so I don't sound like I'm bragging. "It's kinda corny as all hell, but, uh, they branded me 'the Dominator' in the ring." I ignore the soft snort from the kitchen. "So Ky went, 'Dominator? Dom. Dominic.' And I let it stick."

James moves his wheelchair a little closer to me. "Ring? What kinda fighting you do?"

"MMA, mostly." I lean forward. "What about you, Mr. Hadley, you fight?"

"Oh, I dabbled back in high school in boxing and wrestling, but that was a long time ago now."

James accepts a cold beer from Madison, and she offers one to me as well. "You can't drink, right? I wasn't sure."

I wave my hand, declining her offer, and she walks it back to the fridge. "Nope, but thank you."

James arches his brow. "You don't drink?"

"Not that I don't. More that I can't." Resting my elbows on my knees, I clasp my hands together. "I don't have a digestive system."

"Well, ain't that something. Must be nice, not having any grocery bills." James takes a drink.

"Oh, there's a lot of things I can't do. Can't eat, can't drink, can't sweat." I keep Madi in my peripherals. She watches us interact closely while trying to appear busy. "Can't swim."

"You can't swim?" James asks.

"Nope, my mainframe's too heavy. Throw me in the river, and I'll sink right down. But I am waterproof." I'm at ease in these surroundings. "So I don't know. Maybe if I piss someone off enough, we'll see if I can't just walk along the river bottom."

James chuckles as he sips his beer. His movement is stilted. It takes more time than it should for him to bring the can to his mouth. His wrist is unnaturally curved, and the can shakes a little as he holds it, but I don't offer to help or allow myself to appear concerned. Not yet. I want to see him succeed.

He does. "You know, I hear the military is thinking of commissioning BioNex for combat-ready droids. You know anything about that?"

"No, sir. Think they take volunteers?"

James throws his head back and laughs. Madison gazes at her father with a faint, affectionate smile, like she's seeing the man who watched her grow up come alive again. I know, then.

I'm in.

James and I cover all kinds of topics, anything that interests him. I can easily engage him in most every subject, falling quiet and listening when I can't. It occurs to me that half of this caregiving job is just *talking* to him about everything except his condition. He lives in constant reminder of it, unable to escape it. Coddling him, hitting him over the head with his limitations isn't what he wants or needs.

I can see why Madison wanted someone different.

Losing track of time, the sun's gone down before James shows signs of slowing. So caught up in his storytelling of his service in the Ukraine War, I didn't even notice Madison slipping away from the room until she returns, hair damp from showering and wearing a silky pair of soft pink pajamas, smiling appreciatively at me.

"I think it's time for bed, Dad."

"Aw." James gestures to her as he grins at me. "See what I mean? More mother than daughter."

Madison and I share a look. There *is* an almost maternal warning in her eyes telling me not to push my luck with her.

I rise to my feet. "All right. Let's get you upstairs, Sergeant." I don't try to help him maneuver around the furniture as he accelerates his wheelchair. I'm used to moving fast, never slowing down or stopping, but the programming Ky downloaded helps me remain patient. That's new.

I can't let the opportunity pass and have to josh him a little. "Hey, hey, foot off the gas pedal, speedy. This ain't a race."

James cackles heartily as I ascend the stairs alongside the lift that carries him up. "About right."

Madison gives us space. Damn smart woman. If she was flitting around us too much, fretting over him and whether I'm doing things right, it could dampen James's spirits and any connection I might make with him alone. I need to build that rapport on my own, and I think so far I've done a decent job. It's my first day, and already I've cast all uncertainty aside. James's body is fragile, but his mind is still strong. And for all his weakness, he has strength enough to account for it.

For most of my—I don't know how best to describe it. Life, I guess? My three years of existence?—I've been envious of humans. All the experiences they get to have. Eating, drinking. I can have all the sex I want and not worry about disease or knocking a woman up by accident, but I can't be a father. I can't own anything in my own name—not a house or an apartment, not my car, not anything that gives me any kind of legal standing.

But the bright side? I won't be trapped inside my own body, forced to watch as it decays and fails me. I don't think I'll live forever, whatever *forever* even means. But I won't go out like that.

James doesn't need my pity, so he's not going to get any. Madison was worried about jokes, but there's nothing funny about this. I help him get ready for bed, continuing to ask questions about the Ukraine War while changing him and helping him use the restroom. He's cautious, glancing at me here and there, but once he realizes I'm not fixated upon these duties or on any part of his frailty, he seems to relax a great deal.

I help him into bed and cover him up.

He snorts. "Is this where you read me a bedtime story?"

I snicker. "Sure. 'Once upon a time, there was an old man. He was a real smart-ass.'"

James laughs, leaning his head back on his pillow while he rests his arms. "You'll keep Madison company, won't you?"

I shrug, straightening. "Until she tells me to shut the hell up and shut down, I guess I could."

James shakes his head. "She's a sweet girl. Don't let her convince you otherwise."

I turn off the lights. "Get some sleep, Hadley."

I take my time getting accustomed to the layout of the house. The second floor is mostly bedrooms—James has the big master bed and bath to himself, while there are several others, including guest ones. Madison's bedroom is at the other end of the hall, and the door is cracked open.

Rapping my knuckles on her door frame, I glance into the dimly lit room. She's sitting cross-legged on her bed, watching TV.

She raises the remote and shuts it off, looking at me. "Everything okay?"

"Yeah, he's out." I shrug, then motion to her. "You look, uh . . . "

Words escape me. How do I even begin to explain myself? Most of the women I've met after fight nights were more *party all night* than *stay in* type girls, preferring lingerie over pajamas. Somehow, Madison blows them all out of the water without even trying.

"I look . . . " She presses, waiting.

Damn. I was in the middle of a sentence. "You look cozy." Alongside *beautiful, stunning, too goddamn sexy for anyone's good, man or machine.* "That's too bad. Was gonna ask if you wanted to take a walk with me or something. It's a nice night."

She eyes me quizzically, like she's not sure if I'm pulling some kind of practical joke. "Are you for real?"

I had patience for James, but something about Madison's tone has a tendency to irk me. My drives and processor practically bounce off my fucking motherboard whenever I'm near her. What's it going to take to convince this woman that I'm serious?

"Forget it. I'll see you tomorrow." I turn and head down the stairs, shoving a hand into my pocket as I ruffle my hair in exasperation.

Asking her to go for a *walk?* It's rare that I feel stupid. I'm not even sure I'm capable of idiocy. I've driven women all over town, made myself look human by hiding my eyes while taking them to the best nightclubs, the ritziest hotels. And here I am, asking Madison if she wants to take a walk in the middle of the night. I should've led with something else, but what can I say? I've never asked a woman out to do anything before without the implication of fucking each other senseless.

And I don't think Madison is that kind of gal.

"Wait."

At the bottom of the stairs, I glance over my shoulder. She's thrown on a pair of gray sweatpants that hug her hips and a T-shirt and is pulling her hair up into a messy bun.

"All right. Let's go."

She breezes past me with a swing in her step that instantly catches my gaze. I admire her ass.

Fuck. Even her in casual clothes threatens to blow my receptors to hell.

She opens the door, but I catch it, stopping her. "No, no, no, no."

She turns to me in confusion and frowns, opening her mouth as though she means to argue.

I hold up a hand. "You're gonna let me open the door for you, and you're not gonna say shit about it."

She's thrown off. I can see it in her eyes, the way she gawks at me. "You just—"

"Issued a command," I interject casually. "Yep."

"But I thought androids can't do that," Madison stammered.

"Freedom is a thing of beauty." Making my point, I shut the door, open it, and hold it for her as I peer down at her expectantly, motioning through it. "*Now* you can go."

She scoffs, but the way her eyes sweep slightly down my form and right back up again, I know I made a right move, for once.

"A *chivalrous* android?" Impressed, she rests a hand on her hip. "Didn't realize that was a thing."

The thoughts and images pouring through my head are anything but chivalrous. "Better get used to it, princess."

Color twinges her cheeks, but she looks away and heads outside. I follow after, lazily shutting the door behind me with a *click*.

▭

New Carnegie summers are hot, humid, and mosquito-infested, especially this close to the river. The nights are cool and comfortable.

Madison crosses her arms. "So. You got me on a walk. What should we talk about, hmm?"

"That's a good question," I admit as we fall into step together at an easy pace down the sidewalk. We can't go too far from the house, but I can already tell the fresh air seems to be improving her mood from earlier. A quick scan of her vitals shows a healthy blood pressure, a heart rate at ease, and she's not overly warm. "I didn't think I'd get this far."

Her laughter is low, infectious. "That's okay. I didn't think you would, either."

She's witty. Funny, even. "I noticed a few leftover boxes here and there. You're new to the city?"

"Yes. I was born and raised in Philly, actually," Madison says. "We moved to New York for a time, but, well. New Carnegie had the better clinic, the better specialists for Dad's condition. So here we are." She looks curiously at me. "What about you? Where were you, um . . . " She falters, staring helplessly at me.

I can't help but tease her. "Activated?"

She laughs sheepishly at herself. "Activated. Right.

Sorry, just . . . it's weird. It's so easy to forget you're not real."

If it were anyone else, that might rile up my fighting spirit. But she's new to my world, how I work, what I am. I can be patient with her.

"Oh, I'm one hundred percent artificial, but that doesn't mean I'm not real. And I was activated in Maryland for a construction gig down in DC. Wasn't a bad job."

"You in a construction zone," Madison teases. "Bet you catcalled all the pretty girls."

I snort and shake my head. "Nah, had my chip in back then. I was a proper little servant boy. But I got pretty badly damaged a year in. Crane accident. They were gonna scrap me, but Kyrone showed up out of nowhere, paid them for me, fixed me up, and here I am."

"So you didn't have a previous owner that was like, an actual person?"

"Nope. I was a company drone." I shrug. "Got a much better deal going on here."

A few blocks down is a gas-and-recharge station with an old-fashioned ice cream parlor and a convenience store. The lights are always visible, even from the house. That seems to be the direction we're going, and we're halfway there.

"Do you enjoy it?" she asks. "Fighting, I mean."

"Yeah." I slip my hands into my pockets as we walk, unable to contain the excitement in my voice. "Absolutely."

"How'd you get into it?"

"Kyrone. See, he used to be a security guard at the BioNex facility, right? But he figured a time was coming where the company might lay him off, replace him with a droid. So he learns bionic engineering, opens his own shop."

Madison nods. "He mentioned something about that."

"Right. So—you've probably heard of illegal fights, right? Dog fights, et cetera."

"Sure. Aren't those horrible things?"

"Yeah, they are. They're awful," I agree. "You're not human if you hurt a dog."

She likes that, chin lifting as she searches my eyes. "I agree. I always wanted one, actually. Never happened for me." She clears her throat. "Anyway, so . . . fighting."

"Right. Well, Kyrone's got a soft spot for animals too, and his brother is on the police force in Illinois, had just broken up this dog-fighting ring. He suggested refurbishing and fighting droids instead, seeing if they couldn't combat rings like that another way."

"Wow," Madison says, rubbing her arm. "That's really great."

"Yeah, so, it instantly starts gaining traction here in NC." I pause. "You cold?"

"No, I'm fine," she answers quickly. "Keep talking."

I move my hands around a bit as I speak. The guys at the shop always talk with their hands and mouths together, just another habit I've picked up watching them.

"There's no laws against fighting bionics, and when I had my first taste of a real fight, I knew I wanted to keep doing it."

"Really? Why's that?"

"Well, it's an intense sport. A challenge. Much harder than it looks. Dangerous too, but nothing worthwhile is without risk."

"How is it dangerous?"

I touch my chest. "Remember our little punching session?"

"Of course."

"If a human throws a punch at me, it's nothing," I

explain. "If another android throws a punch at me, it could damage my mainframe, my independent battery system, any number of things. We're stronger than you. These aren't little baby fights. Droids can power down permanently in these competitions."

That seems to alarm her. "What happens if you get hurt?"

"Then I get repaired." The tone in her voice has me perking up. "Why, Madi, you worried about me? Already?"

She huffs. "No. I'm not worried. I just—Dad likes you, that's all. If you get damaged . . . Well. Just don't get damaged."

"I'll try not to." My circuits thrill with the slightest electric surge, and my grat drive? Well, it'd be doing a little victory dance up on my motherboard right now, if it could.

Madison cares. It's a start.

At the station, we head inside, and Madison flits indecisively between the fridges and the ice cream, finally picking a glass bottle of cold soda instead. She sets it on the counter in front of a deadpan, college-age cashier, then looks up at me, wide-eyed.

"Shit. I didn't even think about grabbing my purse or my phone . . . "

Androids don't do cards or wallets, and cash has long since died off. Everything's digital. I flick my wrist over the bio-reader, activating my currency chip and pay for the soda in one swift movement. "Don't worry about it."

"You don't have to—"

"Madi." There's a firmness to my voice when I interrupt. "It's five dollars. You can carry that cute little purse around all you want, but you're not paying for your own drinks while I'm around."

Stunned, she stares up at me, blinking furiously. Then,

the gorgeous little pistol who hired me seems to remember she's loaded with attitude. "I don't need a man to buy anything for me."

"*I know*." I glance at the cashier, who's holding back laughter. "I wasn't asking."

She can't seem to decide if she's pissed at me, or if she likes it. I can see that familiar pink glow on her face, but she's glaring. I don't give a damn. Arguing with me over a bottle of soda. This woman is something else.

I love it.

I open the door for her as we step outside. There are a few cars and a big black pickup fueling at the gas pump. I don't pay them any mind, offering my hand to Madison. "Here."

"Huh?" She blinks at me, then hands me her glass bottle. "Oh."

"Not only am I a caregiver, I am . . ." I open the tightly secured pop-off top for her and hand it back. "A built-in bottle-opener."

She takes a drink. "Wow. Got a corkscrew stored anywhere in there?"

"Nah," I reply. The little pistol cracked a joke. I knew she had a sense of humor in there somewhere. "BioNex drew the line at corkscrews."

She laughs a little. "Well. Thank you. For the drink."

"Anytime, princess."

Several car doors open behind us as we start heading back to the house. A quick glance over my shoulder alarms me. I narrow my eyes and continue to walk, but instead of remaining next to her I fall back so that she's in front of me.

Madison's gaze trails over me. "What's wrong?"

"Just keep walking," I tell her firmly.

"Hey! Hey, you fucking garbage can!"

"Stealing our women now, you robotic freak?"

We aren't far from the lights of the gas station. It's all I can do to keep moving as the jeers and slurs continue. Madison constantly looks over her shoulder. At first, she's worried. Then she's angry.

"Leave us alone," she demands, stopping in front of me, her hands balling into fists.

I guide her to keep moving. "Don't engage," I mutter, even as she looks to me and back at them, bewildered and defiant. "That's what they want."

Then something smashes against the back of my head. I whirl around as a half-drunk bottle of liquor shatters onto the pavement.

A group of five men approaches us. One of them has a metal bat in his hands.

"Fuck off," I warn them. "We don't want any trouble."

"Well, that's too fucking bad."

The one with the bat, a kid probably barely past his eighteenth birthday, pushes through his friends, closes the distance between us, and takes a swing at me.

I dodge his wild, uncontrolled strike easily and grab the bat just above his grip, then yank him so hard he lurches forward, stumbles, and falls as I rip the makeshift weapon from his hands and toss it across the street.

The others come for me just as brazenly at once.

"Stop!" Madison's stress is clear in her voice, but these boys are beyond reasoning.

This isn't the ring. There are no lights for me tonight. If this were another android, I could attack freely without fear of retaliation, but these are *people.* And I could devastate them with just a few choice punches. The head, the ribcage, the neck.

I could kill them.

I continue doing my best to dodge. I'm not used to taking on this many opponents at once, but I'm too focused on trying not to wipe the sidewalk with their own blood to avoid being circled. The blows they land probably sting them more than me. Another assailant pulls out an army knife, and he becomes my main focus. I grab his wrist when he takes a stab at me, and with one hard squeeze and twist, I break it. He yelps.

A man punches me in the jaw. I stagger back as he hisses and curses in pain.

I straighten. "You all didn't think this through." One casual uppercut to the jaw, and he's spun around and down for the count.

"Look out!" Madison shouts.

Distracted by the knife, I don't see another man circling me until he attempts to lock me in a chokehold. Breathing isn't something I do, but I doubt he's taking my anatomy into consideration. I'm still holding back. Grunting, I try to escape as I'm struck multiple times in the abdomen. Uncomfortable pulses shoot up my body, lighting up my optics with impact warnings. It looks a lot worse than it feels.

There's a loud crash of glass as Madison smashes her soda bottle down on the head of the man grappling me. While he's disoriented, I peel his arms from my neck and cast him off. Another swings his fist wildly at my face.

But before his punch can even connect, Madison intercepts and hits him square in the jaw.

Furious, the attacker launches at her.

My visual feed goes completely red. "*Don't touch her*!"

I slam him onto the ground and pin him beneath me. My fist connects with his cheek. Then his nose. Bones break.

"Dominic, stop!"

Madison's voice stops me before I land a finishing blow, the anger and resentment that fueled me snuffed out as suddenly as a fire in a downpour of rain. I quickly get up and leave him there, bleeding.

In the distance, the cashier stands outside the gas station, watching with a cell phone in his hands. With three of their friends down, another nursing a broken wrist, and the last without weapons, they rush back to their pickup.

In the distance, I hear sirens.

Madison grabs me by my jacket. "Leave them. We've got to go."

And here I was going to grab her and make a run for it. We sprint down the sidewalk and make it back to the house, then shut the front door behind us.

"Are you fucking kidding me, Dom?"

I wince. I knew I was going to get heat for this. My communication line is open. Kyrone's voice feeds in from his cell phone to the audio receiver built directly in my head.

I slowly pace the house. "It's not as bad as it sounds."

"Uh, actually, it's *exactly* as bad as it sounds. The local news stations are already running with the story from the camera footage."

The last time Kyrone sounded this angry was when I put Montavious, another droid on his team, out of commission during what was supposed to be a practice spar—which, by the way, wasn't completely my fault. Monty is a big dude, almost six-eight. I had to compensate in the ring somehow.

"What the hell were you thinking?"

"Hey, hey, hey," I interject, frowning. "Madi and I were minding our own business. Those dumb shits jumped me. They deserved what they got."

"One is in critical condition in the hospital. You think the law's gonna care if he attacked you first? You don't have any *rights,* Dom. The biggest lesson I taught you was how to take a hit. How are we still having these incidents?"

He makes it sound like this is a regular occurrence. It's still late, so I keep my voice down. "I'm not going to apologize for teaching a couple of Humanity First goons a lesson. Are we done?" I just want to get off the call. I wish I had access to a punching bag.

"No, we're not done. We haven't even discussed how bad this makes me look. I'm supposed to be helping this girl out, not piling lawyer bills on top of the medical ones she and her father already have." Ky's tone sours. "Where is she?"

"Madi's already in bed."

"Good. Maybe this won't feel like a complete clusterfuck by morning—wait. *Madi*? What the fuck?"

"What?" I ask, confused.

"You're on a *nickname* basis with her, now?"

"Yeah, so?" I know where this is going, and I'd prefer it didn't.

"Oh, Christ." Ky groans, and I hear a thump, like he just bonked his head on a wall or a table. "Dom, this isn't *that* kind of assignment."

"I know what kind of assignment it is," I retort with some heat. "And I don't appreciate the insinuation. It ain't like that. She *asked* me to call her that. Anything else?"

Ky is quiet for a moment. "Yeah, there is. You're benched."

"*What?*"

Ky's tone tells me it's not up for discussion. "We have to wait until this blows over. You're gonna stay with the Hadleys until we're sure there's no way they can identify you from the footage. No fights. Got it?" He waits. "I said, *got it?*"

I can fight him as much as I want on this, but ultimately, Ky runs the matches and calls the shots. So if I ever want to be under those shining arena lights again, I better keep my mouth shut. Easier said than done.

"Yeah, fine, I heard you." I slouch my shoulders. "Is that all?"

"That's all. Get some rest. And I better not see you in the news again." Ky pauses. "You know I can't do anything if ACU gets involved."

I set my jaw, nodding. "I know. Good night, Ky. Say hello to Briyanna for me."

"I will."

The call ends. Heaving a sigh, I cross the living room into a corner and straighten, readying myself for standby so I can recharge.

NEW CARNEGIE TIMES

JUNE 1, 2069

PRO-BIONIC ILLINOIS NATIVE RUNNING FOR CITY COUNCIL

When she was young, Rebecca Schroeder dreamed of becoming President of the United States.

"I used to pretend my bedroom was the Oval Office," Schroeder says during her interview with *New Carnegie Times* journalist Amber Rivera. "And my stuffed animals were my Secretary of State, Secretary of Defense. I even stole some of my father's ties so they looked more official."

What started as a childhood fantasy quickly became a passion as she participated in student councils and was elected president of her student body in high school. At St. Morgan State University, she majored in political science and graduated with honors before moving to New Carnegie to continue her work in the finance sector.

That was where she purchased a mislabeled and mispackaged SFX900 V2 prototype named Oliver. After removing his inhibitor—a chip that acts as a sort of restraining bolt—they began what she calls the romance of a lifetime.

"I've dated men. Good men, bad men. Oliver's one of the

good ones," Schroeder says, holding their young son Aaron. "Our marriage is just like everyone else's. We work together. We're a team. Sometimes there are disagreements. Have you ever tried arguing with a man whose brain is basically a supercomputer?" She laughs. "Honestly, sometimes I forget he's an android at all."

Although not formally recognized, unions like theirs are becoming increasingly common. In a new city-wide survey, 8% of New Carnegie residents admit to openly being in a romantic relationship with their bionic assistant, while 20% say they're open to the possibility of artificial companionship. 59% rejected the idea entirely, while 13% were undecided.

"I'm of the mindset that it really doesn't matter what goes on in your bedroom so long as you aren't hurting anyone," Schroeder says. "I'm a consenting adult. Oliver has no inhibitor forcing him to do anything he doesn't want to do, so he also is capable of consent. We're happy together, and I'm not going to hide it."

When asked what she'd like to see improve in the city, Schroeder was eager to share her ideas. Her highest priority? Humanity First.

"I think it's important for advocates of Humanity First and the Pro-Bionic movement to come together and push for change that benefits everyone. I think both sides have far more in common than they realize. I think it's despicable that so many good and hard-working individuals have lost their jobs due to corporations laying off mass amounts of employees only to replace them with androids. That's wrong."

Local social media trends, such as #Schroeder4CityCouncil and #ProBionicBecca are already beginning to surface across multiple platforms.

"We don't have to treat robotics as the next warfront," she says. "Androids were created to help people improve their lives, and they can still do that. It's big businesses that need to be held responsible for these massive decisions that have a negative impact on American families."

Her bionic husband Oliver supports her decision to run for local office. "I think Humanity First has been painted with a broad brush that colors them mostly villainous due to the actions of a few. I've been on the receiving end of that violence myself. In the moment, I could say I was scared. Angry, even, that I was targeted. But that violence was always perpetrated by upset and desperate people who need to point their anger and resentment in the proper direction—high-powered executives who line their own pockets and need to be held accountable for their actions. Not everyday civilians just trying to live their lives in peace."

Humanity First founder Robert Carson, when reached for comment on this curious political development, says, "I appreciate Miss Schroeder's idealism. And it's cute that in her false marriage, she took the name of the inventor of the BioNex androids. That's very cute. But I have strong reservations about her ability to prioritize our communities here in New Carnegie. Androids can't have opinions. They parrot what they hear in an attempt to gain approval from their owners. Removing their chips doesn't do anything except allow them to potentially become violent."

Carson insists, "Free will remains an exclusively human concept. And it always will be."

[3]

Madison

Dominic has been staying with us for an entire week, and I've learned one thing about him, without a shadow of a doubt: he doesn't do idleness well. At all.

Dad isn't so frail that he requires Dominic twenty-four-seven. Without fail, Dom gets him up in the mornings around eight or nine, helps him use the facilities, bathe, shave, and dress, then places him in his wheelchair and follows him downstairs. Dad likes to watch TV while he eats breakfast, so Dom busies himself with the only thing he's got: housecleaning.

I can't believe this.

He's a championship fighter. He's probably used to roaring crowds of people in a packed arena screaming his name in the stands while holding up holosigns with big letters that say *Dominator* or *Kill Him, Dom,* all glowing and sparkling with glitter effects. And here he is on his hands and knees, polishing floors because standing still for more than a few minutes seems like it drives him absolutely batshit crazy.

Restricted to being a bionic assistant, a family caregiver, has got to be his own personal nightmare.

When he told me about Kyrone's decision to bench him indefinitely until he's certain the media's attention has blown over, I agreed with the man completely. A part of me still can't believe that even happened. We weren't doing anything. We were walking. I've never really had any kind of interaction with Humanity First before this. I thought they were just loud, not violent. Not like that.

It's been weighing on me, how much Dominic has to deal with. He loves to fight in his arena, but it seems like he's fighting all day, every day, just to be recognized as an individual. What's more, if he were ever found he'd be killed. *Killed.* It's such an organic word, but nothing else really fits. It's permanently destroying him.

The thought of an android as wholly unique as Dominic being disassembled and scrapped not only bothers me, it makes me angry as I come down the stairs in the later morning hours.

It's difficult for me to wake up before ten. I've been doing it a while now for Dad, but ever since Dominic showed up, they've both been letting me sleep. At first, I appreciated it. I don't sleep well to begin with. But now, seeing how much Dominic gets done around the house and with my father on a daily basis makes me feel a little guilty.

Almost as guilty as I feel when I look at Dominic in ways I shouldn't.

I wanted to dislike him at first. His cocky attitude, the way he gave me a hard time when we interacted one-on-one outside his car. But after that little punching session, the way he slowed me down, how he protected me from Humanity First . . .

I'd be the biggest bitch in the world if I didn't think the world of Dominic after that.

Whenever I see him, my stomach ties itself into a hundred different kinds of knots. One sly grin from him, one simple hello, and I'm strung tight. And that's just his personality. He bends over, and I'm checking out his ass.

What's worse, it seems like he knows, and it drives me crazy. Every chore, everything that used to be mundane, he makes magical somehow—and every single day, it's something new.

Like yesterday, as I was cooking potato leek soup.

He came up alongside me and slid his hand over mine as I held a spatula, stirring. His voice was soft and playful as his other hand lightly brushed over the center of my back.

"Hey, hey, hey. Who said you could cook in my kitchen?"

It's not his kitchen, and he knew it, because the moment I turned to argue with him, he smiled and winked at me, taking the bluster right out of my sails.

"Go sit down. Take a load off. I'll take care of it."

It was delicious as all hell.

Now, I need to stop at the grocery store. He races me to the door and not only opens it for me, but insists on taking me there himself. I try to ignore how luxurious his ride is and how he makes me feel like a fucking princess right up until we park. I try to get out of the car on my own, but he rushes around to intercept me, *pushes me back in*, and shuts the door so that he can open it again and offer me his hand.

"What'd I tell you?" he says when he sees the indignation boiling up within me.

"It's a car!" I protest.

"It's a *door*," he corrects. "I open your doors for you. Me. Not you. Non-negotiable."

Huffing, I take his hand and allow him to help me out. "You realize this is the twenty-first century? Women are capable of driving, opening their own doors, even owning credit cards by themselves now."

"You can drive, you can own credit cards, you can own the whole damn city and run it from a billion-dollar ivory tower for all I care, princess." Dominic points to his chest with his thumb. "But I. Open. Your doors. Period."

Who the fuck taught him to be so chivalrous? Kyrone? And where does Kyrone get off teaching Dominic to behave like this?

More importantly, why the hell do I love it so much?

Damn you, Kyrone Johnson.

I relent because I worry arguing further will only make it obvious just how much my heart skips when he does that. But when his eyes sweep over me, I'm pretty sure he already knows. Some kind of scan he can do. His pupils always shutter and narrow like camera lenses when he does it.

So not fair.

At home, he walks around like he's not just God's gift to women but to *me*, and goddamn it, I kinda hate that he is. When I start a load of laundry, I have to stop him from getting it out of the dryer to fold it.

"No! Nonono. I draw the line at my clothes," I protest, trying to push him out of the way. "I'll do it."

Damn him. He's built so solidly I can push all I like, but he's only going to move if he *wants* to.

He gives me a look. "Nah. I don't think so. James is napping, and I gotta have something to do."

"T-then—" I stammer as he picks up the laundry basket filled with my clean clothes. "You can—clean the floors!"

"Nope, did that already."

"Wash the dishes? The kitchen counters? Vacuum the carpets?"

"Done. Done, and done."

"Mow the lawn?"

"I did that hours ago, *and* I fixed your lawnmower for you. It was broken," Dominic replies, shifting the basket so it's underneath his arm, resting on his hip. "Try again."

He tries to walk past me, but I get in his way. He tries again to move around me, and I cut him off.

"I will fold my own clothes, Dom," I insist stubbornly.

We stare each other down, his stark white eyes searching mine. Then he smirks, shrugging. "Whatever you say, princess."

Bristling, I push against his chest as he attempts to walk past me—which does absolutely nothing on our hardwood floor. I'm wearing socks. He chuckles as I slide backwards. Desperate, I jump on his back, and he doesn't even stagger, only slightly hunches over and pauses as I adjust my position with my arms around his shoulders and my legs around his waist.

"Give me those clothes."

"Is this supposed to deter me?" He glances over his shoulder at me. "Because it isn't working." He carries me piggyback-style to my room with my laundry basket still in his hands.

Yep. I've definitely made a mistake. Bad enough he keeps doing everything right, but now I can feel just how powerful he is through his shirt, and it's got me thinking about him in ways I've been trying to avoid.

This is the first time he's been in my room, and he *tsks* as he sets my laundry basket down on the floor and straightens, me still on his back.

"Madi, Madi, Madi. The bed isn't made, you got clothes tossed around the floor—"

I scowl. "I like a lived-in look."

He's grinning. "You better get off me and let me do my job."

"Not a chance." I tighten my legs around his waist. I don't know what's gotten into me, but I feel . . . playful. Rowdy. He pushes my buttons so easily, I want to see if I can do the same.

That's what I tell myself, anyway. Deep down, I know the truth.

I just want to be close to him.

Dominic's brows quirk with mischief. "You got five seconds, or this piggyback ride's gonna turn into a rodeo."

I squeeze him tighter defiantly in response, gazing at him and all but daring him to do it.

"All right. Just remember you asked for it."

Then my father starts coughing in his bedroom.

Dominic's lighthearted teasing fades to concern, and I lower myself down as we both hurry to check on him.

"Dad? Are you okay?" I call. "What's wrong?"

Dominic opens the door and finds Dad struggling to sit up. He quickly helps him do so, patting his back.

"Take it easy, Hadley. Got some heartburn?"

"A little bit," Dad says with another cough.

Guilt courses through me, harsh and cold. For just a few minutes, I let myself forget everything else. I shouldn't have done that. Dad comes before me, before my sister, before everyone. He needs me. I can't be flirting with anyone—man or android.

Kicking myself inwardly, I head back to my bedroom to fold my clothes alone.

The remainder of the afternoon was quiet, but dinner is anything but.

So maybe Dominic's little commentary on my room worked, and I tidied up. But just a little. It keeps my hands busy and helps me work through any lingering feelings of reproach before I head downstairs. Dominic's already got supper on the table and has quickly caught on to all of Dad's favorite dishes: New York strip steaks, buttered garlic asparagus, potatoes au gratin, and homemade apple pie.

Apple fucking pie. With the little crumbles on top.

This man bakes. *Are you kidding me?*

But it's not his cooking that's got my attention. It's Dad.

I sit down next to him and listen to him and Dominic talk for the better part of an hour. Not only are they talking, but Dad laughs, smiles, and tells stories like he used to. The fog of what the next few months could bring seems temporarily lifted, and it wasn't me who did it.

It's Dominic.

Machine or not, he's bringing out this side of my dad again that makes me both nostalgic and content. Dad's eyes shine with amusement as he makes jokes. For a little while, at least, I forget he's even in a wheelchair, and everything is how it should be.

Then Dad's gaze finds mine, and he smiles. "You like music, Dom?"

Oh no. Moment over.

Dominic follows his eyes and nods, canting his head at me inquisitively. "Sure, I like music."

"Any particular type?" Dad continues, despite my pained expression, silently imploring him to stop there. But no, Dad's got that twinkle in his eye. He's gonna keep going.

Dominic shrugs. "All kinds. I don't know. I haven't really thought much about it."

"Dad—"

"What about classical?" Dad deliberately ignores me. "Madi here plays piano."

There's amusement in Dominic's face. "Does she?"

"More than plays," Dad says proudly. "She's a master. Went to the New England Conservatory of Music, and the professors couldn't say enough about her. She performed abroad in Finland, Czechoslovakia, Austria, England, China. Was going to perform in New York."

My cheeks are pink with embarrassment as I avoid Dominic's stare.

"No kidding?" he says. "I mean, I saw the piano and a few pictures here and there around the house, but I didn't realize you were so well-traveled."

I rub my shoulder, sheepish. "I don't really like to talk about it that much."

"Play for him, Madi," Dad urges. "Come on."

"It's been two years," I protest, shifting uncomfortably. "I wouldn't be any good."

"Nonsense. Like riding a bike." Dad won't give it up. People think I'm stubborn, but I learned it from him. "For me."

Dominic remains quiet, simply studying me. He doesn't tease me or try to pressure me. If he would have started making jokes or taunting me, I probably would've said *hell no*. But no. The usually talkative, playful android who's made himself at home in our house? Perfectly well-behaved.

And when Dad pulls the *for me* card, I know I can't say no. Not to him. I never could for long, but certainly not now. *Dammit.*

"All right. But if you think I'm going to play you an entire concerto, you're out of your mind."

I head to the study, where my grand piano awaits me, and hear them follow.

Playing piano isn't just a hobby or even a profession; it's a ritual. Sacred. I feel less like an accomplished musician and more like an imposter; a sinner who's been away from church too long.

I sit down on the bench, already perfectly placed where it should be in respect to the piano itself. I slowly lift the sleek black lid and let my fingertips brush the ivory keys. My father's wheels come to a halt, and Dominic lowers himself into a chair in the hallway opposite of the open study.

My heart skips in my chest, stomach seizing with a fresh helping of nerves. I can't explain why, not at first. My dad has listened to me practice and perform, whether I'm terrible or tremendous, from the time I first began this musical obsession on a tiny electric keyboard.

Then I realize I'm not nervous because of Dad.

It's Dominic. I can feel his eyes on me.

Steadying my breath, I play the only piece that comes to mind: Gershwin's *Rhapsody in Blue*. Simple enough, right? The piano doesn't just make noise when I touch it, it sings beautifully, responding to every tap of my fingertips.

But I'm rusty. It's been too long, and when I make mistakes, I hear them and grit my teeth in frustration. Even though it's been years, my inner critic rails into my self-esteem, telling me I shouldn't be this unpolished. My room might be a bit of a mess, but when it comes to my craft, I'm a perfectionist. It just isn't good enough.

After playing for a little while I pause, letting the music taper off into silence. When I turn to look at them, Dad looks happy. Even proud. A familiar satisfaction settles over me—that I'm doing my best for the both of us, and despite everything, my music can still make him smile.

Dominic is different. When our eyes meet, he seems to realize his mouth was slightly ajar and quickly shuts it. He straightens in his chair.

"That was wonderful. I've missed that," Dad says.

I thought it was horrible. Sometimes I wonder if he'd say the same thing if I just rolled my face across the keys. But hearing it still gives me little wings, makes me sit just that much taller.

"Thanks, Dad."

He looks to Dominic and smiles. "What do you think?"

"I . . . uh." Dominic doesn't seem to have words. I'm not sure if that's a good or a bad thing.

"Can you play?" Dad continues.

"What?" Dominic blinks. "Uh. No."

"You sure about that?" Dad asks. "Come on, you're a droid, right? You should be able to do anything."

"Well, sure, but some of that downloadable content and programming costs extra. I never really thought about using my hands for anything other than . . . " Dominic almost sounds nervous. "Breaking stuff."

"Why don't you try? Go sit with Madi."

"Uh, okay." His usual swagger is replaced with an awkward sort of amble as he comes to sit on the long piano bench alongside me. "But she played from memory, so . . . "

Dad's never going to let up, so I smile sympathetically at Dominic and go to one of the many bookshelves aligning the walls, then pull out a piece of music.

"This is *Für Elise* by Beethoven."

"Is that difficult?" Dominic asks, focusing curiously on the music in my hand.

I open the pages and set it in front of him. "Eh, it's kind of the basic bitch of the classical world," I tease, sitting down next to him. "Figure we start you off small."

But Dominic doesn't need small. He stares at the notes printed on the page. His pupils shutter, zooming in and out. Then he begins to play.

His movements are stiff, like he's reverted from his natural state into something more mechanical. Every note he plays is correct, so perfect on his first try that it frustrates me. He breezes through the piece without pause or stumbling even once. When he's finished, he looks at me expectantly.

"How was that?"

"Great," I say shortly, rising and heading to the kitchen. "Just great."

"Madi." My dad reaches out for my hand.

I let him take it, squeezing. "I need a minute, Dad," I tell him softly. "It's fine."

But as I continue past him, I hear his heavy sigh behind me.

In a few moments, Dominic finds me as I pour myself a glass of water, wishing it was wine.

"What was that?" he demands.

"Nothing," I retort, setting the glass in the sink, forcing myself to relax again. Short fuses usually aren't my thing, and I can think of a thousand reasons why I'm wound up tighter than any screw, but I know it's wrong to take it out on him. "It's just—"

He folds his arms, staring me down. "Just what? Spit it out."

"I've worked my entire life to play piano as well as I do. I've earned my skills," I snap before dialing it back again. "You can just download a modification and play the music without a single fucking mistake. It's infuriating."

Dominic scowls at me. "I can't help what I am." He gestures to me and all around him, scoffing. "Not my fault I was created this way."

"No, and I know that," I counter heatedly. "But when a machine can play just as well as I can in a shorter amount of time without even practicing, what's the point of me playing at all?"

I'm being unfair. This is a tantrum; I know it is. And the moment the words escape my mouth, I feel like I'm slapping him in the face.

He clenches his jaw as he looks at me. "Anything else?"

"No, there's nothing else."

He's already turned and headed away from me, shoulders square, looking like he's ready for a fight. I hear him speaking with Dad before the garage door opens and slams shut.

It takes me a little while to cool down, and the house is quiet that whole time. Dad went into the garage, following Dominic, and it feels like I have the entire place to myself.

Which doesn't help me feel justified in my little outburst at all. If anything, the silence reminds me of how much of a bitch I'm being. So Dominic can play piano with a single download. So what? The more I think about it, the more unnatural, tense, and robotic he seemed while doing it.

Perfection isn't just in playing the right notes. Perfection comes from becoming the instrument itself. And no two instruments are the same. His ability to plunk out a few measures without tripping up doesn't negate the fact that I have talent.

And call me arrogant, but I *know* I have talent. Unless all those teachers and mentors have been blowing smoke up my ass, which I hope isn't the case. Otherwise, Dad wasted a *lot* of money.

I owe Dominic an apology. I'm not the sort of person who never says sorry. I've got pride, but not *that* much.

I suck it up and put on my big girl panties as I wander downstairs to find that walking, talking, sexy refrigerator so that I can apologize. It takes me a moment to hear them in the garage, right where I left them to go sulk. I slowly open the door and find Dad showing Dominic his most precious possession.

His black 1969 Ford Mustang.

They've got the hood up, and Dom's poking around in it, looking like a peasant boy in a king's treasury, his eyes wide with appreciation and reverence, while my father just sits back and soaks in the visiting android's wonder.

"We've gone over every spec," Dad says, "but you still haven't told me what you think."

"What do I think?" Dominic scoffs. "This is the most beautiful damn car I've ever seen. Hell, it's more beautiful than mine. I hate that. How much do you think it's worth?"

"Oh." Dad shrugs, playing humble. "Since it's fully restored, probably . . . I don't know. Half a million. Maybe more, since she's a hundred years old."

"Incredible," Dom mutters, gently closing the hood.

I refrain from commenting. The Mustang has been a source of tension between me and Dad. I've watched his retirement funds slowly drain away from medical bills. Selling the car would definitely give us some breathing room, but Dad refuses. I learned quickly to not bother arguing with him about the car.

But even thinking about the car boils up more tensions in me as I think of my sister Chloe. That's how it is with me. I'll be minding my own business, and *bam*. I remember how much I loathe her. Thankfully, for my own sanity's sake, she doesn't pester me every day. In fact, she hasn't all week, since she's off in her own little world.

She'll argue about that car with Dad until she's blue in the face. Self-inflated, irresponsible, and air-headed at the same time, she's not concerned with Dad's bills.

No, she just wants the five hundred thousand dollars, which she and her useless husband would blow through easily within a year, knowing them. *Fucking brat.*

I can't think about her. She makes me too angry. She always has. Dad tried his best with her, but she was always getting into trouble. She's got no ambition, no passion for anything except desiring wealth, but doesn't want to work hard for it. She's never accountable for her own actions, it's never her fault, and I can't forget our blow-out fight back in high school where she stole my wallet. When she left for college, she cut me out of her life, then returned to it when it suited her and pretended like nothing happened. Didn't even apologize.

Funny how that works. I'm the younger sister. I should be reckless one, splurging through my money.

But no. She plays Dad like I play my piano, asking for money occasionally when she needs it, without actually giving a damn about him. I can only stand by and try to keep my mouth shut.

Dad is so proud while Dominic slides his hand over the smooth metal of the Mustang's roof.

"I planned to give it to Madison as a wedding present,"

Dad says wistfully. "Lots of memories, restoring this beauty. Thought she and her future husband, whoever he is, might appreciate it. Dreamed about tune-ups with a grandson or a granddaughter too. But unfortunately, no man has measured up quite yet for my youngest. She'll probably end up selling it." He glances at me as he steers his wheelchair toward the ramp, heading back into the house. "Ain't that right, Madi?"

"I don't *want* to sell it, but it might be a necessity, depending on how everything gets settled," I admit, not wanting to talk about that sort of thing because it means admitting Dad will be gone when it happens. "I love it as much as you do."

Dominic turns to face me, quietly horrified, brows up and mouth open as he shakes his head. "No, no, no, no. You can't sell this."

"I won't, if I can help it," I say with a defensive little shrug. Once Dad is inside the house, I continue. "Look, I'm sorry about earlier. It's not your fault how you're made, nor is it your fault I haven't touched a piano in like, two years. I shouldn't have reacted the way I did. It's just . . . "

I shift uncomfortably under his gaze. The way he looks at me, so intensely, makes me feel like I'm under a spotlight I can't escape from.

"Just what?" he asks, folding his arms.

I'm not getting out of this, so I struggle through it. "Imagine, you've done all of this hard work and training for your fights, right? And then someone else comes in, and they don't even have to train. They just outdo you. In one go. How pissed would you be?"

"Pretty fucking pissed, I guess," Dominic assents quietly with a little nod, then waves a hand dismissively. "Except I didn't outdo you. You said it yourself. I was playing the basic bitch of piano songs."

"Piece," I correct.

"Eh?"

"It's not a piano *song*. Songs have words. It's a piece. Pieces are compositions without—you know what? Doesn't matter. Point is, I'm sorry."

"Yeah?" Dominic smiles down at me. "Well, apology accepted."

Everything goes quiet between us for a moment. We both stand near the slumbering Ford Mustang. I didn't realize it, but I took a step forward while we talked, and there's less than an arm's length between us. Why am I so tempted to make things happen, all from a single look? It'd be so easy to push myself against him, put my arms around him, kiss him senseless. Those vibrant white eyes of his and his self-assured smile are like a porch light, and I'm an oblivious little moth, getting drawn in without realizing.

"You want to try again?" I ask softly.

"Try what?" Dominic pauses. "Oh, the piano? Depends. Are you gonna storm out again?"

I can't help but laugh at that. "I was being a brat, wasn't I?"

"Yeah, you were, but that's all right. Not like I've never been an ass before. Sure. You wanna try again, we'll try again."

When we sit down at the piano together on the same bench, I become increasingly aware of how his proximity affects me. I keep expecting he'll smell like plastic and metal, but he doesn't. He smells like the slightest hint of soft, woodsy cologne and fresh clothes. I guide his hands to the keys, then brush my fingers against his back.

Explaining how to move with the music and how to

let it move through him earns me a skeptical, somewhat flat look, but he watches me play, then tries again. When I show him a video of some of the greatest concert pianists, he sniffs importantly, mocking their seriousness, and exaggerates his movements until my sides hurt from laughing.

Before I know it, I'm leaning against the piano, tears in my eyes, smiling so wide my cheeks hurt. Wheezing, I can't seem to stop giggling.

"I can't. Oh, god."

"You can." His smile fades into something less impish and more sincere. "You should. Play more, I mean. It makes your old man happy."

Brushing my hand through my hair and ruffling it out of my face, I bashfully shake my head.

Dominic doesn't stop there. "And I've never heard anything like it before. It's beautiful."

Hope pierces through the veil I've concealed my own passions with. "Really?"

"Yeah. I mean, it isn't my usual hip-hop." His shit-eating grin returns, as does my soft laughter. "But watching you play, I see what he meant."

I cautiously close the keylid. "What do you mean?"

Dominic gazes into my eyes and locks me in, and I realize too late how dangerous he is, sitting next to me like this.

His voice softens, lowering. "I'd go to every concert. Every performance if it meant getting to see you and . . . " He frees me when he glances toward the piano. "Watch you do something you love."

I blush when his attention returns to me. "You're just teasing me now."

"No, I'm serious. I mean it. You lit up the room when

you were playing before. I couldn't keep my eyes off you." He pauses. "I still can't."

My heart catches and flutters, and I look away. "That's actually really sweet, Dom. Thank you." I rise from the piano bench, then organize and put the sheet music in its proper place.

"You're welcome," he says, and behind me, I hear him getting up too.

"So, um . . . " Filling in the silence is all I can think to do. "Anything from Kyrone about the footage?"

"No. Nothing yet. I'm just supposed to hang tight." He moves around the piano and rests his elbows on top. His gaze is on me, but I'm too chicken to look up, scared that if I do, I'll say things that betray this ache taking hold of me.

"I'm sorry it happened. It shouldn't have. That walk was a dumb idea."

"No," I protest quickly. I have to meet his eyes now. "It wasn't. I enjoyed it. They ruined it, not you. I still can't believe that happened. It feels so surreal when I think about it." I swallow, resting similarly across from him. "Does that . . . does it happen often?"

Measuring me in silence for a moment, he nods a little. "I've had run-ins with Humanity First before. A few times, downtown mostly. Usually just kids thinking they're tough, wanting to beat the shit out of something to make up for Daddy losing his job. I've never had to go hard like that before because it's normally just me, or maybe me and Monty or one of the other droids. I never wanted you to have to deal with that."

A pregnant pause resting between us tells me more than perhaps even he knows. It's almost as though he's warning me, telling me that this could be my life if I get involved, that I should turn around and run while I still can. I don't know why I'm considering it. I don't even know what I want. A relationship? A hookup, just to get it out of my system?

But he's not just uncharacteristically quiet; he's vulnerable, standing here with me, talking about this. And I can't let it go.

"It isn't fair," I say. "You've done nothing wrong. Nothing to deserve that hate."

Dominic barks a short dry laugh. "Yeah, well. When do people ever need a reason to hate each other, let alone bionics?"

"They shouldn't hate you," I reply with a vehemence I didn't realize I was holding in. "I don't hate you."

"I know you don't hate me, Mads. It's all right."

Mads. Madi. However he says my name, I like it. Unable to think of anything more to say that won't get me in trouble, I move around the piano toward the hallway. Part of me hopes he won't let me escape that easily, that he'll come up behind me and press kisses to my neck.

He keeps his distance. "I'm gonna go check on James. Thanks for the music lesson, princess."

There it is again. The nickname he has for me, and my favorite above all else. At first, I thought he was being mocking or derisive, but the way he calls me "princess" actually makes me feel like one. But it's clear words are all I'm getting tonight.

I turn to face him, masking my disappointment. "Anytime."

NEW CARNEGIE TIMES

JUNE 22, 2069

BIONEX OPENS IN CHINA

BioNex's market continues to grow internationally as their first store opens in Beijing. Store clerks were greeted by a long line of excited customers and quickly sold out of their inventory.

To keep up with high demand in the country with the highest population in the world, BioNex announced its intentions to open factory facilities in China, in full compliance with government regulations, at its latest press conference.

Releasing bionic assistants in China has been a long and arduous journey for the American-based company, but newly appointed CEO Blakely Hamilton has high hopes.

"We are very excited to be doing business with our friends overseas," she says. "Our goal is to see a bionic assistant helping families live their richest lives in every home, not just American."

The androids in Beijing are modeled differently in order to stay in compliance with regulations. They cannot have any realistic sexual anatomy, and any kind of misbehavior with an android is a reportable offense.

“China takes the family unit very seriously,” said Li Jiang, head of the highly anticipated BioNex-China project. “Bionic assistants are meant to support families, like servants, and afford more family time, not confuse or tempt people into deviancy.”

Members of the Humanity First anti-android group are taking to social networks to condemn BioNex’s decision to extend its reach abroad.

“It’s sad,” Robert Carson, the group’s founder, said in a recent podcast. “My old friend had a vision, and he saw it through, despite all my disagreements with him in the process. Then that vision, that dream, started getting warped by corporate greed. And now we have a multi-billion-dollar company looking for ways to get richer without any concern for the negative affects they will have in every community they touch.”

[4]

Dominic

My gratification drive is a particular sort of monster.

Cooking? Meh. I can do it, but it's boring. Cleaning? Boring twice over. There are only three instances of service where I feel completely satisfied.

Fighting, caring for James, and spending any time at all with Madison.

It's week four on this assignment, and I can't return to Ky to even talk about fighting until this weekend. James is good as of right now. I've been doing everything I can for him, and we've definitely got a rhythm to our routine. At the moment he's just finished breakfast and is relaxing while watching the news.

I'm only half listening, but all of the media's bluster from the night of the attack seems to have died down. Right now, any and all focus on BioNex and androids is in regard to their opening in China, as well as the inhibitor chip bill.

"What do you think about that, Dom?" James calls over his shoulder.

"Hm?" I turn off the water and dry my hands with a towel. "Which part?"

"The chip thing," James says. "You gonna let 'em stick that back in you?"

"Hell no," I snort, and he laughs at my response.

The feisty princess of the house is still asleep. She seems to enjoy it when I call her by that name, so I'm not stopping anytime soon. She comes down from her ivory tower, as I like to call it, around ten every morning, which will be an hour from now. It can't come soon enough. Whether she comes down in her pajamas with her hair tied up in a messy bun or fully dressed with all her makeup on, she is an absolute bombshell. Twenty-four hours a day, seven days a week.

And just one look into those warm brown eyes is enough to knock me down for the count.

She's been playing piano on her own, every day after dinner, and every time I hear her music I have to stop, listen, and watch her in her element. When she plays, she's at her happiest, and it lifts James's spirits, too. She likes to call me over when she's finished and have me play alongside her, coaching me on how to make the music move through me.

I go along with it because it gives me a few precious moments of Madison. The way she talks about, thinks about, and hell, *breathes* piano is the way I feel when I'm in the ring on fight night. Oh, I've already downloaded everything there is to know about performing piano. I can list off every famous composer, every piece, and every key.

But I don't want her to stop talking, so she doesn't need to know that.

It's been busy the past few days. Madison has been

anticipating the arrival of the porch materials for the new patio she's having a nearby building company install in the backyard. James loves to be outside and grill during the summer, and she wants to make sure they have an opportunity to do so while also increasing the value of the house.

I don't like thinking about that part or the fact that Madison has to anticipate losing her father and having to pick up the pieces of her life when he's gone. I wish there was a way to reverse the inevitable. It's hard to believe that no cure has been found for these diseases, but androids like me are a thing. I'm not complaining about existing, but I hope someone out there at some point gets their priorities straight.

The installation company dropped off all the wood necessary this morning, along with the regretful news that they won't be able to start for a few weeks. They leave all the paperwork with me to give to James, including the blueprints for the new patio.

James grumbles as he looks it all over. "What a bunch of horseshit. What are we paying these guys for, aside from ruining my lawn?" The company deposited the materials on the grass and quickly hightailed it to their next delivery. James looks up at me. "Wait a minute. You said you were a construction droid, right?"

"Yeah."

"Take a look at this." James offers me the blueprint with some strained effort, which I take and scan over while he rolls back to the living room, intent on enjoying his TV binge. "I have tools in my garage. Any tool you can think of, I definitely got it. Think you could build it?"

"This?" I call back to him. "Easy. I could set this up in a day."

"Set up what?"

Turning, I see Madison descending the stairs and have to keep my mouth shut. Because god*damn*.

She's wearing a yellow sundress, cut to her knees and showing off her legs. Those legs. I want to kiss every inch of her body, starting from there. This woman is going to blow my circuits. I don't bother hiding the fact that I'm giving her the onceover because I can tell—the way she's looking at me, playing all coy like she just rolled out of bed like this? Yeah. She knows she's an all-you-can-eat buffet for my eyes, and I devour every inch of her.

"Don't worry about it." I don't want to talk about home improvement jobs right now. "Where do you think you're going dressed like that?"

She tucks her long brown hair behind her ear. "Dressed like what?"

Oh, she's pushing all the right buttons, and she's doing it on purpose. I've had about all I can take. An entire month with her in close quarters like this has got my gratification drive doing overtime. All I want to do is back her up against the wall, brush my thumb across those soft pink lips, and—

A loud, jarring series of knocks abruptly puts an end to that hungry train of thought. "Hel*looooo*?"

Madison looks away from me in confusion, then rolls her eyes as she bites back a groan. "Oh no."

"What is it?"

The expression on her face can only be described as *help me*. "It's my sister and her kids."

She pulls here and there at her dress as though suddenly self-conscious and composes herself before opening the door with a thin smile.

"Chloe. Hi."

I'm not sure what I was expecting, but not this. Chloe is completely different than Madison in appearance, although a brief scan indicates they have a similar facial structure, and they stand fairly close in height.

Where Madison has long brown hair and brown eyes, Chloe is fake blond and rocking the soccer-mom, let-me-speak-to-your-manager mom 'do, all buzzed with spikes. She's slender and small-boned, with tiny wrists dripping with bracelets of pearls and rose gold. She wears aviator sunglasses, and her belly's on display and studded with body jewelry.

"Oh my god, Madison, hi!" she exclaims as her two school-age children push past her gigantic black leather purse. She gives Madison a big hug, one that's only half-heartedly returned. "Look at you. So pretty! You've put on some weight, but nothing a walk here or there won't fix."

"Wow, thanks," Madison says flatly.

I narrow my eyes. Being an android and a male, I'm no expert on female communication but that sounded like a back-handed compliment. From Madison's body language and diagnostic scan, she's not happy about this visit whatsoever.

Chloe's children surge past me and head for the living room, where I hear James greet them happily.

"What are you doing here?" Madison pats Chloe's back awkwardly before pulling away.

"Ryan's at his union meeting, remember?" Chloe says. "Obviously, I was going to stop by. Like we talked about."

She notices me and stops right in her tracks, eyes widening. "Oh my god, you bought an android!" Her gaze rakes over me, down then up. "A *gorgeous* android. Mm-mm-mm. Gotta have that eye candy when you got him working around the house for Daddy, huh?"

Madison, annoyed and exasperated, gestures to me. "This is—"

"Dominic," I interrupt, offering my hand. "I'm the resident caregiver."

"So you are." Chloe wiggles her shoulders. "Wanna give me some care later?" She laughs boisterously, patting my arm. "I'm kidding." She gives me a flirtatious wink before going to greet James in the other room.

Half amused, half annoyed because of Madison's frustration, I rest a hand on my hip. I have no interest in watching her walk away and turn back to Madison. "So that's your sister."

"Yep." Madison purses her lips. "That's Chloe. And my niece and nephew Ryleigh and Anton."

Her hackles are up, so I try to bring them down a bit. "She looks nothing like you."

Her eyes snap to meet mine and flash with ire. "What does that mean?"

"Relax. Put your claws away, kitty cat, and simmer down." She frowns at me, and I continue. "I said what I said, but I didn't mean it like that, and you know it. She doesn't look like you. Or James, for that matter."

The tension ebbs as Madison forces herself to unwind. "I dunno. Dad says she looks more like Mom, I guess."

I've heard James talk about his wife Sarah. Always bittersweet and nostalgic, never angry or resentful. In the hopes of keeping his spirits up, I never pressed. Now, however, I don't think I can ignore it anymore.

"Where is she?"

"Dad never told you, did he?" Madison smiles at me. "Figures. Classic Dad. Gotta keep up that tough front."

"You don't have to tell me." I listen as the kids overwhelm their grandfather with stories of their school and home life in the other room, talking over each other all at once.

"No, it's okay," Madison says. "Mom died shortly after I was born. Something about an uncommon infection that no one really anticipated. Least of all Dad. One minute she was fine. Next minute he was planning her funeral and trying to figure out how to care for a newborn and a toddler by himself."

Chloe's kids catapult past us at full speed, only to skid to a halt when they realize who—more precisely, what —I am.

"Whoa, holy shit!" the little boy exclaims, which takes Madison by surprise. "A real android!"

"Language, Anton," she scolds.

"Sorry." Anton doesn't sound sorry. He reaches out and prods my arm. "Ha, he feels like a person. Can you shoot lasers out of your eyes?"

I snort. "Uh, no."

"Can you punch supervillains?"

"Maybe."

"I can punch supervillains." Anton proceeds to punch my hip and wince. "Ow."

"That's what happens when you punch the *superhero*, kid." I smirk. "Now who's the villain?"

"Tell you what. Why don't you two go downstairs and check out the toy room, huh?" Madison opens the door in the corridor, and immediately they rush downstairs. "Don't run and don't hit." She shuts the door. "That's going to be an F5 tornado by the time they leave."

"Authoritative." Amused, I pass her and head toward the living room.

"Please," she scoffs, following me. "That's probably the most authority these kids have had in years."

Even though Madison isn't thrilled about Chloe's visit, James seems quite pleasantly surprised to see her in contrast. As Madison settles down on the sofa next to him, I head into the kitchen, where Chloe's going around opening cabinets.

"Looking for something?"

"Oh, just a glass for water," Chloe says.

When I glance at Madison, she shakes her head at me and makes a drinking gesture.

Don't let her find the liquor cabinet. Got it.

"Let me get that for you," I offer, going into another cabinet and pulling out the glass she needs. The conversation resumes between Madison and James. He tells her a couple of his friends, other Ukraine veterans from out of state, are planning a reunion trip in New Carnegie to come see him.

While they're distracted behind us, planning food and drink for his old war buddies, Chloe sidles up alongside me in front of the kitchen counter.

"You know . . . " She brushes her hand subtly over my groin. "My husband says androids don't count."

I lift my brows as I set the glass of water in front of her. Her proposition and touch initialize nothing. "Here." Unfazed and uninterested, I put distance between us as she winks at me, drinking deeply.

I go to stand behind Madison, remaining at ease and pensive James catches up with his older daughter. I'm surprised at myself more than anything. A month ago, Chloe was precisely my type, the kind of woman I'd take for a ride out in my car, give her a night on the town, and a romp or three between the sheets she'd never forget.

I don't usually go for married women. Once I see a ring, I tap out. Not interested in a brawl with an angry husband or hurting families. I'm free from restraint, but that doesn't mean my programming to care for mankind isn't still intact. But I can't say I haven't ignored an indentation on a ring finger before when the opportunity was just too good to pass up.

Reminiscing about my lifestyle before this assignment, how casual and uncaring I was, enjoying my newfound freedom with a life-in-the-fast-lane mentality makes me want to cringe. Before Kyrone, I was just a drone. I built homes, businesses, whatever. It didn't matter. Activation, work, standby. Wake up, work, standby. For an entire year until that crane smashed on top of me. I didn't know what the hell a family was. That wasn't my job.

But thinking about James losing his wife, raising two girls on his own. Witnessing how dedicated Madison is, putting her own dreams, ambitions, and enjoyment on the back burner, willing do whatever it takes to take care of him. That's a kind of devotion I've never known.

The long list of girls I've sampled in the past are all a blur, but Madison? Madison's vibrant and in color, at the forefront of all data. My every action revolves around her.

That's when it hits me like a clock to the jaw.

After this assignment is over, no matter how long or how short it ends up being, she'll always be imprinted in the back of my mind. It's not possible for me to forget her. Hell, with how stubborn she is, I doubt a factory reset would unseat her. She's burned in my memory drives.

My systems go nuts whenever I'm around her. I don't know what it means to be devoted to someone, but with a woman like her?

I wouldn't mind trying.

My gaze trails to Madison, lingering on her for a while, when I notice James looking at me. A slow, knowing smile tugs at his lips, and I quickly look away, excusing myself from the room to find something, anything to do to keep my hands busy and my thoughts distracted.

It doesn't work.

Madison Hadley has gotten me so hooked I didn't realize it until far too late. Her attitude, her compassion, her talent; everything about her captivates me. Even the surge I feel in the ring can't compare to being near her.

Chloe doesn't stay long and herds her kids back out to the car. I descend into the finished basement-turned-toy-room. In a matter of less than an hour, the place looks like a hurricane blasted through it. As I pick things up and put them away, I let my thoughts wander to Madison again.

I have a vivid imagination. I always have, ever since Ky repaired and reactivated me. I won't pretend like I haven't pictured Madison naked under me, on top of me, in front of me, every which way. But it isn't sexual fantasies that's driving my processor right now.

I'm thinking of what it'll feel like, saying goodbye to her, after this assignment is over.

And I don't think I can.

In fact, I know I can't. I won't be able to do it.

Saying goodbye means James is gone, and I've gotten so attached to the guy, I struggle picturing that too.

As I finish up cleaning after the bomb the kids set off in the basement, I hear the keylid open in the study as Madison begins practicing. I never really cared much about music, before now. I barely thought about it at all.

Now I can't hear a single tune without her vision in my head.

A call coming in across my dashboard rings, lighting up my visual feed. It's Ky.

I quickly answer. "What's up?"

"Good news." Ky never leads with pleasantries, one of the things I like best about him. "I think it's safe for you to come back this weekend. Think you could make it tonight for some practice? The championship fight is on for tomorrow night."

"I'll be there." My circuits surge at the prospect. Being under those lights again, the crowds, the rush. I'm more than ready for it.

I head upstairs and stop when I find Madison in the study. She isn't just playing today. She's got blank sheets of lined paper up on the music rack. She plays a few chords before writing them down and occasionally grumbles in frustration, staring at the keys beneath her fingertips.

"I didn't know you compose music too."

She turns to me, exasperated. "Usually, it's stress relief, but today it's . . . I'm really sucking today. I used to write piles and piles of this, and I can barely get out a few lines."

"Well, don't force it." I shrug, sitting next to her on the bench. "Knowing you, it'll come out eventually."

She smiles apologetically. "I'm sorry about Chloe. She seemed a little *friendlier* than perhaps she should've been."

Understatement of the century. But as she and Chloe are already on the rocks, as I'm beginning to suspect, I decide to refrain from telling her precisely how right she is.

"Sorry to disappoint her, but she's married. And even if she wasn't, wouldn't matter."

"Why's that?" Madison asks, but the way her breath catches, I can tell she already knows my answer.

I give it anyway. "I got the hots for her sister."

Madison's face turns red, and she scoffs, harmlessly shoving against my arm with a soft laugh. "Stop."

And there it is. The arm touch. As if the handful of other times we've found excuses to be in each other's personal space weren't indications. I'm not worried about whether or not she enjoys it.

She may be struggling with putting her music down in writing, but her body language is composing entire symphonies just for me. And I am all ears.

"So." I give her a little shoulder nudge. "Ky just called me. Once James is all set, I'm gonna head out for some practice tonight, come back afterwards. Tomorrow's the biggest match of the year. You wanna come?"

"And watch you fight?" She perks up curiously. "Really? That's okay?"

No reluctance or disinterest. As though I needed another reason to be glitching over this woman. "Absolutely. I'll have to win, knowing you're watching me."

"What about Dad?" she asks.

"What about me?" James hollers from the living room. "I know you're not using me as an excuse to get out of a well-earned night out, Madison Rose."

"Madison *Rose*, huh?" I murmur quietly. "Listen, he's right. Don't worry about it. I can have one of Ky's other droids come on over. Montavious. He used to be a hospital assistant down in Georgia."

"You sure?"

"Course I'm sure. It's me." My broad hand practically swallows hers as I take it and squeeze lightly. "I want you in the stands, Madi. Will you be there?"

The way her entire face lights up with such a small gesture sends thrills along my circuitry, gratifying me in ways I haven't experienced. And all from a gorgeous smile, her hand in mine.

"I'll be there."

NEW CARNEGIE TIMES

JUNE 27, 2069

PROPERTY MODIFICATION LEGISLATION THROWN OUT: RIGHT TO MODIFY APPROVED WITH NON-LEGAL EXCEPTION

In a surprise motion, what has been referred to as the "Anti-Customization Bill" or "Android Bill" has been dismissed by the House of Representatives on a bipartisan level, with Republicans and Democrats voting against the document's many proposals surrounding android regulation.

Included in the bill's 57 pages are dozens of new measures, including a ban on removing the bionic inhibitor chip located in almost every android's "brain." This inhibitor chip renders them incapable of disobeying orders for any reason, as well as ensuring they cannot react violently to a potentially hostile situation.

Alongside fining and forcing independent bionic repair shops to acquire certification for operating outside of BioNex was another proposed ban on making android sports illegal, which local shop owner and trainer Kyrone Johnson believes was a singular attack on his business.

"Oh, I know they hate me," Johnson says. "I'm literally the

embodiment of everything they didn't want to happen. I have a bionic wife. First thing I did when I got her was take out her inhibitor chip—but let's call that like it is. It's a slave chip. Then I opened my shop, and they hated that too because they can't make money off me and my clientele. And then I put together a winning team for the New Carnegie chapter of what we like to call BFL. Bionic Fighting League. The android fights."

Johnson says, "I can't speak for every guy who runs in the fighting circles, but my androids all choose to do what they do. I don't force any of them to do anything. And like I've said before in another interview, 'cause y'all keep coming around, the police department knows who I am. They're aware of what I do, and even they've had to admit that there's been less dog fights, less nasty things like that in the city since we started."

According to Becca Schroeder, who is currently running opposite Joan Bell for City Council, there was one regulation conspicuously missing from the Android Bill.

"All of these rules, and not one of them holds any consequences for a corporation or a business that chooses to replace its human workforce for an artificial one. No fines, no limitations, no nothing for the multi-billion-dollar corporations who are throwing our economy into disarray in order to line their own pockets," Schroeder says. "So basically, this is a BioNex bill that was intended to protect BioNex's ability to make money and punish those who try to make money too. That's it."

Republicans voted against it, citing it was an infringement of rights, whereas Democrats echoed Schroeder's sentiments.

A representative from BioNex did not return *New Carnegie Times*'s calls for comments.

[5]

Madison

I keep trying to tell myself it's not a date.

Technically, it isn't. He's going to be in the ring, I'm going to be watching. There's no chance of cuddling, kissing, holding hands on a walk, dinner, flowers. But I can tell this means a lot to him by the way he's talked about the sport.

He's passionate about it. It's something I never thought possible for an android. Yet, somehow I can appreciate that a hell of a lot more than guys who are *passionate* about sitting on the couch and yelling at the game on TV while playing in the fantasy leagues.

There's a big difference between the guy who watches the dream and the guy who lives the dream. I can find lots of men to devotedly stare at football games or well-rehearsed wrestling matches every weekend without fail. It's not that there's anything wrong with those kinds of guys, either.

But being able to be in the stands, cheering Dominic on? That's a whole different level.

For the past few weeks, I've been doing my best to pretend Dom isn't the first thought in my mind when I wake up and the last one before I sleep. I've avoided acknowledging that he's the reason my desire to play the piano is returning, slowly but surely. Music, the one thing I've loved ever since I was a child, has become enjoyable for me again.

And it's because he sits next to me and lets me metaphorically push him around, hanging onto my every word. He is the reason.

Dominic isn't just an android; he isn't just the caregiver for my father anymore. He's become my muse. The highlight of my day, every day, with his panties-off smile and the way he teases me and gives me a hard time just to make me laugh.

So this may not be a date, but I sure as hell am prettying myself up like it is one. After my hair is done and my makeup is on point, I stare at my closet before I finally pull out my smartphone and shoot him a message.

Hey.

There's a brief moment of quiet, but as I stare at the screen, I see him formulating a response far quicker than someone could if they were truly typing. He mentioned messages come straight across his visual feed, but that's incredible for me. I haven't been on the dating scene for a while, but when I was, it was a miracle if the guy could reply in the same hour.

Hey, gorgeous.

Butterflies are supposed to be for teenagers, but I guess my stomach doesn't remember how old we are.

I type along the holographic screen quickly. ***I've never actually been to one of these things before and I have no idea what to wear.***

Funny you should bring that up, Dominic replies. ***Apparently, this match is gonna be televised since they threw the BioNex bill out the window.***

"Holy shit," I mutter to myself. *Televised?* ***Are you worried someone will recognize you?***

No, not really. Ky determined that the video was taken from too far away, not enough focus to really identify me. And the guys who attacked us would have to incriminate themselves in order to talk. I'm not scared.

I hope he's right. Dominic doesn't strike me as the type to stay hidden for long, no matter what. ***Wow, TV, though. Sounds like a big deal.***

Yeah, I guess it is. Kinda like Ky and the other sponsors are giving BioNex the middle finger. So, whatever you feel like wearing for the cameras.

Feeling foolish and with a smile tugging insistently across my lips, I can actually hear Dominic's voice in my head when I read his messages, I know it so well. Every lilt, every cadence. It's there, and I can't seem to make it stop. I start typing a response without really thinking it through.

What would you like me to wear?

A longer pause than usual. ***Oh, all sorts of things. Probably nothing too crazy in the stands tonight, though. I gotta be able to focus on the droid I'm***

knocking out, not the knockout in the crowd. I'm technically breaking rule number one already.

I suppress a giggle. ***There are rules?***

Sure. Ky's got a system. No looking at girls, talking to girls, or fucking with girls until a match is over. And definitely no texting girlfriends beforehand. You're gonna get this Pinocchio in big trouble.

I re-read that message a dozen times, butterflies doing delighted little somersaults in my stomach. *Did he just call me his girlfriend?* I'm trying to focus here, hesitant after learning of these rules. I want to go, but I want him to win.

Should I stay home?

No, no. I want you there. Rules are meant to be broken, right? He sends me another line. ***You didn't say anything, by the way.***

What?

I can practically hear his teasing voice in my ear. ***I called you my girlfriend. You didn't correct me.***

The butterflies in my stomach are playing pinball at this point. I read that line over a dozen times, then another dozen, feeling like my feet have left the ground and I'm floating.

Another little flash of text appears beneath it. ***You really know how to make a man sweat it out, and I don't even have that capability.***

I snap out of my reverie, my cheeks hurt from grinning so wide. I rub my face a little as I fire it off. ***Maybe I wanna hear you say it before I make a decision.***

My phone rings. I lift it to my ear.

"You're really gonna leave me hanging, before the fight

of fights, huh?" He clicks his tongue. "Madi, Madi, Madi. You're killing me, here."

His voice, smooth as silk, has me weak in the knees.

"Can't have that." I pace around my room, so filled with energy I can barely remain still. "Can we?"

"Nah, we can't. So was this all an elaborate ploy to hear my voice, or do you miss me already?"

"Maybe." I sit down on my bed, biting my lip. "Or maybe I wanted to hear you ask me out properly so I can think about it."

"Is that what you want?" His voice lowers an octave, flirtatious, rich. Sexier than anyone organic, and he knows it. "You want me to ask you out right now, like this, over the phone?"

"No," I counter, flopping back on my bed and staring at the ceiling, cheeks aching while I continue smiling like a moron. "I want you to ask me out after you win tonight."

"Oh yeah?" He doesn't betray any kind of disappointment or any inclination that I'm slowing him down. It'd surprise me if I did. Dominic is a freight train of self-confidence, if nothing else. "All right. You got yourself a deal. This win tonight? It's gonna be for you."

"I believe you." My body aches for him, allowing myself this small admission. "I'll see you soon."

The call ends, and I lie on my bed a moment, letting the truth sink in.

Win or lose tonight, it doesn't matter. Dominic has me cornered on the ropes, and I love every minute of it.

Deciding to go with a classic that can never go wrong, I pick a little black dress with an asymmetrical skirt that shows plenty of leg, something I've caught Dominic glancing at more than once. I keep my hair down and go simple on the jewelry, then check myself out in the mirror.

That's when I realize I haven't been out in ages. I barely recognize the woman staring back at me.

Montavious arrives an hour before the fight. He's a tall android with brown skin and long ashen synthetic locs pulled out of his face, a salt-and-pepper goatee, and a friendly smile.

"Heya, Madi," he greets me warmly. "Where's James?"

I step aside so he can come in, motioning to the living room down the hall. "Oh, he's getting all set for Dom's fight on TV with his friends."

"Oh, good!" Montavious sounds excited, keeping his shoes on but wiping them on the doormat politely. "I didn't want to miss it. You can head out whenever. I've got things under control here."

When he greets the other men gathered around in the living room with a hearty and boisterous hello and introduces himself without fear or mechanical politeness, I know that he's just like Dominic—different, and in the best way.

Kyrone is one hell of a miracle worker.

I peek my head in. Dad flashes a smile as bright as I've ever seen as he shares old war stories with his friends over cold beers.

"Madi!" he exclaims. "Look at you!"

His old pals all turn, and in an instant they're cheering for me and clapping, hyping me up. I've known a lot of these guys since I was young. They've popped in and out of my life since I was old enough to remember, and I'm embarrassed by the attention.

"Where are you going all prettied up?" Matt, or "Sergeant Matty," is a heavily tattooed teddy bear with a peppered beard and a do-rag.

"Our android is fighting tonight," James says with some pride.

"No shit?" They all gawk at him. "Which one?"

"The Dominator."

It's *so* hard not to laugh at the cheesy title. I don't get how men love stuff like this, sometimes. But seeing them all excited to watch Dominic makes me proud, and something about the way Dad looks at me tells me he knows precisely why I picked the dress I'm wearing, why my hair is done up, and why I look and feel like a million dollars after a few playful texts.

Dad treats Montavious like another one of the guys, and everyone else follows suit. Sergeant Matty even hands him a cold one as though he can drink it. Poor Montavious stares at it for a moment before setting it to the side on a table.

Folding my arms, I listen to Dad gush about Dominic, and it warms me. He doesn't see a robot. He sees a man, like I do.

You aren't just born a man, he always used to say. *You're made one.*

Reassured about leaving him alone, I glance at my phone, which lights up with a few notifications from Chloe, and promptly ignore them as I head out to my car. Nothing is going to foul my mood tonight.

As I drive downtown, I replay my conversation with Dominic over and over again in my head. I let my mind wander, fantasizing about his mouth against my ear instead of my phone, my body pressed into his. What it would be like to be pinned down beneath him, my legs wrapped around his waist, grinding on his—

Okay, whoa. I snap out of it, shaking my head, heat

between my legs. I should probably save that train of thought for after the fight.

I find a place to park on a ramp and take a glass elevator to the ground floor, my gladiator stilettos clicking against the pavement as I follow a trail of spectators heading for the arena. Near the doors, there's a ticket booth and I stop in my tracks, unsure. I could text Dominic, but with a half hour until the match starts, I don't want to bother him.

Fuck, I'm rusty. Should've definitely checked with him about tickets.

I approach the booth and wait my turn. The attendants there are both female androids wearing sparkling sequined emerald minidresses, looking like they should be spinning signs, posing for a game show, or strutting new fashion on a runway rather than handing out tickets to attendees who appear to be mostly men. One of them sports long eyelashes and hot pink fingernails and chews bubblegum as she gives me a winning smile.

Androids can't eat, but I never thought of one happily chewing gum. I guess that wouldn't matter to an android. We don't swallow it, either.

"Heya, honey. Did you call ahead?"

"Sorry, I'm not sure how this works." Sheepish, I look around. "Did Dominic leave a ticket for me?"

Both of them perk up. The other android woman, platinum blond with porcelain skin, speaks up and takes me by surprise with a deeply Southern accent. "Beg pardon, buttercup, but did you just say Dominic?" They both lean in, peering at me intently.

Their scrutiny makes me nervous, and I'm unsure why. I laugh awkwardly. "Yes. He's helping my father with—"

"You're Madi!" the blonde exclaims excitedly, taking

my hand without warning as she squeaks giddily. "Oh my sake's alive, this is so exciting. Brandi, take over for me."

"Sure," the other android says, turning her attention to the next group of people in line as the blonde bionic lets me go and comes around.

"I'm Briyanna," she introduces herself with a bright white smile.

Briyanna. The name sounds familiar. I've heard Dominic mention her while on the phone with Kyrone. My apprehension skyrockets. He called me his girlfriend so easily over the phone. It would make sense that he's been with ladies before, but I never really thought about it.

"Madison Hadley," I reply, holding out my hand to greet her and hoping she's not an ex-girlfriend.

"Dominic's been gushing about you ever since he got back," Briyanna says, beaming. That's when I notice a sparkling diamond ring on her ring finger, which throws me completely for a loop. She catches me eyeing it, holding it out for me to inspect. "Pretty, ain't it?"

"It is," I manage, taking her hand and turning it this way and that.

"Ky put a ring on it three years ago, and he hasn't regretted it since." Briyanna pulls out a small tablet. She has me read off my phone number. My phone dings with the image of a ticket. "There ya go. Just wave it around the fellas at the gate if you need to leave and come back. You'll be let through without any trouble."

"Wait. Kyrone?"

Briyanna peers at me with her bright white eyes. "Yeah. Ky's my husband."

My trepidation washed away with some relief, I stare at her in surprise as she takes my hand without any further warning and leads me to the door. *Married?*

I didn't realize androids could marry at all. I've seen snippets and headlines here and there about people who identify with the Pro-Bionic movement, who declare they have artificial partners or spouses, but the undercurrent of derision in those stories made me skeptical.

"You're gonna be sitting in the very front, right up close to the ring so you can see everything," Briyanna says. "If you see Kyrone, pretend you don't. He gets pretty worked up about these matches."

She waves at two bionic attendants dressed in sharp black security uniforms as she brings me on past, ushering me through.

"Have fun!"

Astor Arena is completely transformed when it's filled to the brim with crowds of people. The rumble of thousands of conversations fills the dome as I clutch my phone and carefully descend long stairs, passing rows upon rows of other bystanders. When I finally find my seat, 15A, I set my purse down and take a long scan of the venue while trying to keep my mouth from dropping to the floor.

It's a full house, packed in even as far back as the nosebleed section. There are cameras, reporters, shimmering lights everywhere. Androids wear sleek black and green athletic tops that sport a flashy grunge logo of Kyrone Johnson's business, Tin Man's Heart, across their backs. They hold up harmless, transparent holo-launchers at the crowd and let T-shirts fly. Some fans hold up holographic signs that flash, scroll, and come alive with messages like **Kill Him, Dom** or **#DomiNation.** Many wear merchandise of their own, supporting their preferred fighter.

Green seems to prevail in the stands—Dominic's color. They're all here for him. I even catch a glimpse of three girls wearing neon green crop tops, each of their bellies painted with a letter of his name: D-O-M. I had no idea his fan base was this extensive, and it's all sinking in.

He never told me just how popular this sport has become, or how he's practically a celebrity. I knew he was passionate, but I never knew there was a demand for his skill like this. When I heard "underground," I pictured a few dozen men huddled together in a garage, watching two droids punch each other like those antique Rock 'Em Sock 'Em Robots you see in museums.

Holy shit, was I wrong.

I bite down a swell of pride that quickly turns into a fluttering of nerves as my gaze catches the countdown of a shimmering holographic timer. It's two minutes until go time, and the lights are going down. People clap, cheer, and whistle as a spotlight follows a trim, well-dressed android swaggering down an aisle, flanked by two sporty female bionic referees. Four large plasma screens anchored into the walls come to life as little camera drones hover, twirl, and soar in the air above the crowds and rotate around the ring, capturing every larger-than-life moment.

"Ladies and gentlemen." The android's voice booms into a wireless button microphone attached to the collar of his shirt. "Artificials and organics alike, welcome to the very first televised match of the newly founded"—he pauses, looking around as a roar of excitement begins to climb—"and totally legal Bionic Fighting League!" He holds out his arms as the unified and deafening cheer takes over the entire stadium.

I applaud with everyone around me, caught up in the exhilaration of this discovery. The rush of simply being in the stands supporting Dominic's passion is the only feeling that has ever matched the thrill of performing piano onstage.

The android continues. "For those of you new to our flourishing sport, would you like to meet our fighters tonight?"

The roar in response has me beaming so widely my cheeks ache. The lights dim and turn green. Drones dart over us to focus in on the tunnel on the far left of the arena.

"You know him as the USA Bionic Champion of 2069, located right here in New Carnegic. This BN7979 has yet to be defeated in the ring. He's mean, he's green, he's the ultimate fighting machine—"

It's so cheesy, like the entrances you'd expect from vintage wrestling entertainers where everything is rehearsed, but everyone eats it up. I guess in some things, humanity never changes. Meanwhile, I wonder if Dominic ever told me he was undefeated, and I come up blank. He's never boasted, so hearing someone else boast for him fills me with pride.

As though he's mine. And right now, I want him to be. More than ever.

"He's the destroyer, the demolisher, the one and only—"

Dominic comes through the tunnel and into view and instantly, the response is deafening.

"*Dominator*!"

I applaud and cheer with everyone else as Dominic takes his time making his way to the ring, a cocky, winning smile on his face. He lifts his fist, and the crowd goes wild for him again. He wears green fighter shorts and a champion belt, his powerful body on display for everyone to see.

He's absolutely gorgeous, and he knows it. He hoists himself into the ring, slipping between the ropes and does one quick circle, greeting his fans and seemingly feeding off the energy they emanate. Then he goes to his corner and readies himself.

Then his gaze finds mine, and he brightens with the biggest smile he's ever given me before looking away. Kyrone and a handful of other androids are on the ground in his corner. I recognize them as Ky's team, the ones who trained with Dominic when I was first brought to the ring. They're all decked out in variations of green outfits, all with Dominic's name on their backs. Ky, in contrast, looks fine wearing a pinstripe suit and tie. If he's nervous, he doesn't show it.

"Mind if I sit with you?"

I glance to the side as Briyanna stands alongside me. I smile brightly at her. "Of course not."

"It's exciting, isn't it?" she calls over the roar. "This is a bigger turnout than we hoped for."

"You must be so proud of Kyrone."

Briyanna tightens a hoodie around her sequin dress, bouncing on her heels a little. "I am!"

The lights dim again.

"Our challenger tonight is also undefeated. This BN7989 was built solely for fighting and nothing else. He made his debut in 2067 in the New England underground circuit. He's won matches in Brooklyn and across the sea against bionics in Belfast, coming all the way from Boston, Massachusetts—"

In sharp contrast to Dominic's simple and rather upfront introduction, this one is over the top. A montage of high-definition fights plays across the screens under a reddish filter while crimson lights skim over the right tunnel and scarlet sparklers erupt in fountains of fire.

"It's the one, the only Irish Hurricane—"

I'm only given a few moments to ponder how an android can possibly be an Irish anything before Dominic's opponent saunters into view and is greeted with a similar level of enthusiasm, roaring and shouting and cheering from the crowd. There are some jeers, but they're drowned out quickly. The sport is so new that it doesn't appear anyone has really adopted a loyalty to fighters and their cities yet. Everyone's just excited to be here.

Slack-jawed, I stare at the visiting fighter as my wonder fades to worry. Call it my horrible Americanness because I'm used to cliché leprechaun mascots, marshmallow cereal, and badly done accents in a variety of Irish pubs. When I think Ireland, I think short sturdy redheads with feisty attitudes. This droid? He's easily six-six, broad, and larger than any bionic I've ever seen.

Dominic looks like he could lift a truck. This fighter looks like he could lift a navy carrier.

I huddle with Briyanna so we can hear each other talk over the noise. "What's the story on this guy?"

"Custom build," she replies. "Real name Connor. His owner's a rich guy up in Boston with a hardon for boxing glory days. He's over there. See him?" She points out a man similarly dressed to the nines with black-and-white wingtip shoes, watching as Connor climbs through the ropes into the ring. "He took him to Belfast to train him against the bionics there because they've had an artificial fighting league since BioNex opened in the UK. It's silly, really."

"Why's that?" I ask.

Briyanna looks at me with a derisive snort. "There aren't any hurricanes in Ireland."

Dominic doesn't appear even the least bit intimidated. If anything, he's more determined than ever to bring him down. I expect nothing less, and the pride in my chest just keeps growing.

This man wants me *to be his girlfriend?*

A referee in a black-and-white striped shirt—he looks human, but I can't see his eyes to be certain—stands between them and addresses them briefly as they square up. The two androids stare each other down with hardened expressions, touch knuckles, then the match begins.

Dominic and Connor instantly put distance between each other and circle around the ring, fists up as they bounce and shift, always moving. Dominic attacks first with several quick jabs. His challenger takes a defensive position as he tests him, looking for openings.

Then with a flurry of strikes Connor's on the offensive, and he's gaining ground. Dominic raises his arms to protect himself, and I can hear every hit of Connor's fists against Dominic's arms, metal upon metal.

My body is tense, and I wince with every punch.

With each hit Dominic takes, I feel as though I'm getting hit with him. I clench my muscles, my fists flexed. I know this is a sport, but I never anticipated the stress of watching him. Ky shouts supportively at Dominic as the two droids continue to swipe at each other.

Dominic gets in an uppercut, and Connor takes a step back but retaliates ruthlessly. He jabs harder, faster, and Dominic's having trouble keeping up. Then Connor has him backed against the ropes.

"Come on, Dom!" I call, trying to ignore one of the announcers sitting at a table nearby.

"We're getting a taste of exactly why Connor is called the Hurricane!" the android announcer says.

Ky's still shouting as the two androids clench each other. Connor gets one, two, three hits to Dominic's ribcage, and I cringe. Briyanna shouts next to me too, more fired up than I am.

Then Connor headbutts Dominic, and a whistle shrieks as Dominic staggers and falls to the ring floor. The referee quickly cuts between them. Everyone around me makes a unified noise of shock and distaste, jeering at Connor.

"That's against the rules," Briyanna calls angrily.

I stand on my feet, expletives flooding my mouth, and I don't bother to bite them back. Dominic pushes himself back up, glaring at Connor while the so-called Irish Hurricane smirks, even while the referee berates both him and his owner, then calls for a break.

Kyrone slips between the ropes with one of his engineers, who tends to Dominic. Briyanna and I sit back down.

"Is he all right?" I ask as the engineer dabs him with ice water rags.

Portions of his synthetic facial skin are pulled away to reveal the metal skeleton beneath. I'm instantly taken aback when I see his plastic exoskeleton underneath for the first time. I saw droids like this in Kyrone's shop, but it's different. It's Dominic. He looks so unearthly without his skin. Sleek, smooth, black and blue, but his eyes glow. He's almost alien-like without his synthetics.

"What are they doing?"

"Androids don't sweat." Briyanna smiles reassuringly at me. "But if we push ourselves too hard, we can still overheat. Think of any computer you've ever owned, right? Laptops getting too warm, towers shutting off. The same thing applies here. If Connor gets Dominic to overheat and shut down, he'll win the match. They're just making sure his cooling systems are still operating correctly to prevent anything like that from happening."

"Can they kill each other in these matches?" I ask

worriedly, watching Kyrone coach Dominic on strategy and wondering what they're saying.

"They used to when we were underground," Briyanna replies. "But there weren't any rules back then. It was just a free-for-all. And it depended on who you fought with. Now that bionic fighting is being recognized as a sport, they've had to civilize it. And head-butting is definitely against the rules. Mr. Hurricane knows it. He got the memo." She glares at Connor as he refuses to sit down, pacing on his side of the ring while his suit-and-tie owner looks on smugly.

Kyrone claps Dominic's shoulders, and he gets to his feet after the engineer has finished his diagnostic. I can read his face well enough. He's just as angry as I am.

"Come on, baby," I whisper under my breath. "Destroy him."

The bell rings and again, the two fighters clash. Dominic isn't on the defensive this time; he swings and punches and swerves, narrowly missing strikes above his neck. He manages to sweep a leg out from under Connor, and Connor falls while they grapple and punch at each other.

Dominic lands a few more blows before the bell rings again. The referee pries them apart. Kyrone looks pleased as he addresses Dominic again while his engineer runs another quick diagnostic. On the opposite end of the ring, Connor looks forward neutrally as his owner barks at him, red-faced. I take that as a good sign.

Two more rounds like this, and the winner is still anyone's guess. The fifth round is the most brutal of all. Both droids all but charge each other as they land and defend strikes before Connor manages to trip up Dominic. They wrestle and struggle against each other.

A chant goes up on my side of the stands: "Dominate, dominate, dominate!"

I bite my lip and chew my nails, just wanting this over with. I'll be his girlfriend happily, win or lose, and I want him to win, but I also don't want him beaten within an inch of his life, artificial or not. I second-guess myself, wondering if I have what it takes to really be with him when this is his passion, the life he's chosen. This won't be his last fight. There'll be more, and then even more after that.

Can I really watch him take more hits like this?

But no. If I let on that I have any uncertainty, if he glances over at me and sees doubt in my face, the fight will be over.

I quit my own calling, disappointing my father and more importantly, myself.

I'm not going to quit on Dominic now.

And just like that, it's as though my own decision channels into him. Dominic overpowers the other android. He's got Connor in a hard grip that the other droid can't get enough traction to get out of. His opponent's arm is in a precarious position.

"Not looking good for the Irish Hurricane." I can hear the announcers' trepidation.

"You know, it appears the Dominator is using his own size against him."

"A good hour of sound thrashings from Connor, and it appears Dominic has had enough, finally living up to his name."

"I tell ya, I don't want to be one stuck with the repair bill after all this!"

Then there's a loud metal *crack*, and Connor's neutral visage breaks into one of confusion and pain—I'd no idea androids could actually *feel* pain—as Dominic dislocates his shoulder. Connor is down for the count, finally tapping out. The entire arena leaps to their feet as Dominic disentangles himself from his enormous competitor and drags him up onto his feet. He lets Connor go, and the referee lifts his hand up as everyone around me screams for him. Briyanna and I bounce up and down with joy, embracing each other. Drones fly overhead for close ups of him.

"The Dominator, the first champion of the newly founded BFL in the very first legal and broadcasted bionic fight on American soil has secured his place in history. What an amazing turn around for this small and scrappy droid—"

"Come on," Briyanna says, beckoning me. "I'll take you behind the scenes."

"Is that allowed?" I ask, following her.

She beams at me. "I'm the coach's wife. Everything's allowed."

It takes a little while, but security lets Briyanna through as she brings me back around through the crowds of people funneling out of the exits and into the back area, where there's a locker room, a restroom, and a tech and lighting room for the arena and storage. Kyrone stands there with the other androids and his engineers, all talking excitedly and preparing for a press conference.

Dominic, oddly enough, is not among them.

Briyanna squeaks, "Sugar!"

Kyrone turns and catches her when she launches herself at him. He twirls her around and kisses her deeply. "We did it. Did you see him out there? He put on a hell of a show." His eyes find mine, but he doesn't seem all that surprised. "Well, if it isn't Miss Hadley."

"Congratulations!" I shake his hand. "You must be so proud."

"More than proud. I'm officially being hailed as the father and founder of the Bionic Fighting League," Kyrone declares. "Beat all the bigwigs to it and locked it in before they could."

Briyanna's voice rises another octave. "You mean—"

Ky's smile is almost wolfish in nature as he scoops her up again. "We're rich, baby girl!" He dips her into a deep kiss, which turns into several more, their smacking loud, playful, and unapologetic.

I look away at the blatant show of affection to be respectful, an anxious fluttering in my stomach. I'm glad I'm not the only one losing my mind over somebody artificial. "Do you know where Dominic is?"

"Oh, you just missed him. He ran to the restroom." Kyrone manages to pull his lips away from his wife to answer me, motioning down the hall. "Just to catch a look at himself in the mirror. He always has to look good for the ladies." He smiles at me and winks. "Or lady."

I make my way down the hall and pause by the men's restroom door, trying to decide if I want to risk just going in. It doesn't seem to be busy, so I doubt there's anyone using the facilities. It's been a long time since I snuck into the boy's bathroom. A good sixteen years or so. *Wait, how old am I?* I'm far too wired to do math in my head right now.

I'm about to steel myself and wait when I hear a very recognizably female voice coming from the other side.

I wonder if I'm hearing things at first, because there couldn't possibly be a girl in there with him right now. Could there?

Kyrone mentioned he always looks good for the ladies, but I didn't give it much thought. I'm not insecure by nature, but my hackles are up and gripping me tightly. I reach for the door, controlled by the dreadful rock in my gut.

I have to be imagining things.

Frowning, I open it and walk in, then turn a corner past several vending machines embedded in the walls that project holographic advertisements for things like pomade, stain removal, cigarettes, and condoms.

Then I stop in my tracks, heels cemented to the floor. My stomach plummets, and I can no longer doubt my own eyes as I'm robbed of the air from my lungs. I don't hear myself gasp, but I must have because they turn to look at me.

Dominic is pushed up against a urinal by a busty blond woman in neon green pants and a bra to match. She's already cast her top to the floor and is pressed against him. He breaks away from her and sees me. His eyes are wide. Her red lipstick is smeared across his lips.

"Madison," he says, startled.

I stare at them in shock for a moment while this woman smirks at me, unashamed and triumphant, before I turn on my heel and head for the door.

[6]

Dominic

"No, no, no, no. Madison!"

My biocomponents were cooling, but now they churn through my body again, up and down my surging circuitry, not from pleasure or the promise of a good fight but from panic as I pull away from the blond woman and follow Madi.

"Wait!"

Swiftly turning the corner and barging into the hallway, I see her already stalking for the exit, her heels clicking loudly against the white reflective floors. "Madi!"

I break into a jog, catching up with her as the exit door swings open. She doesn't try to slam it in my face or even acknowledge me as I call her name. She just keeps walking.

"Dom!" Kyrone's voice booms down the hall. He looks at me in confusion. He's got his arm around Briyanna. "The fuck are you doing? You got an interview in five minutes."

"Yeah, well, they're gonna have to fucking wait," I call back sourly.

"Dom!" Kyrone calls again, bewildered, but I've already left him behind, chasing after Madi as she heads for the nearby parking garage.

This is not how I wanted this night to end. I had a whole thing planned. Sure, the fight got a little dicey and a loss would've dampened my spirits, but I would've gone through with it all anyway: give a few interviews, snap some pictures with Ky and the crew, maybe even with Madison, if she wanted to.

But winning the match wasn't supposed to be the highlight of tonight.

Winning the girl was.

"Wait, wait, wait." I skirt in front of her to bar her path, and she tries to circle around me. "Madi, listen to me."

"Don't." Her voice is curt and sharp, like the tip of a knife. "Just don't."

"It's not what you think." I keep stepping in her way. "Madi, why would I ever—"

"You're such a fucking asshole," she huffs, glaring right up into my eyes without an ounce of fear. "Move!"

Scowling, I glare back at her. "No. Not until you let me explain."

"There's nothing to explain!" she fumes. "You're just a —a—" She's so furious she can barely talk. "A walking garbage can, i-in a nice package! I know human men can behave that way, but you? I thought you were different!"

All of her fire, that anger, everything is now what I love most about her. I just don't particularly like it aimed at me.

"That isn't fair."

"Oh, I'm sorry, the pretty girl's tongue down your throat isn't fair?" she snipes back. "Look, if I wanted to go out with a shallow piece of shit, I could've just downloaded a dating app and met up with the first dick pic sent my way."

"None of that was me." Exasperated, I don't know what to do to make her listen, but I can't back down. I'm not going to let her walk away without explaining myself. "Let me prove it, Madi. Please."

She glowers, folding her arms with her jaw clenched. "Ten seconds, then you walk away from me and tell Kyrone our little agreement is over."

"All right, fine."

Ten seconds is more than I need. I've already been gathering the data from my visual feeds, compiled it into an attachment, and shot it off in a message to her phone. I motion to her purse as it begins vibrating.

Muttering curses to herself—about me—Madison opens it up and takes out her phone. She sets the camera to holo-project in front of her, and proceeds to play the video I just sent her from my viewpoint.

I was staring at the mirror after changing into my gray pinstripe suit and silky green tie. Ky wanted me to look like a regular gangster for the cameras, and I planned on delivering, but that wasn't why I wanted to look good tonight. I have reservations at the Moonlight Ford, a ritzy place right on a historic riverboat for drinks and dancing. I was going to take her out for a drive, having the perfect scenery in mind, ideal for the places I imagined our conversations would go.

Most importantly, I have James covered by Montavious. He was in on the whole thing, practically begged me to do it.

"She might never admit it," James told me this morning, "but spending time with you makes her happy. Happier than I've ever seen her."

Those were the thoughts on my mind as I fixed up my

synthetic hair and readied myself for the cameras, willing myself to get through all the PR so I could get to the good stuff.

That was when the stall door slowly creaked open behind me, and a woman with long blond hair and a big D painted across her stomach came into view, grinning like a cat at me with cherry red lips.

"Hey, baby," she cooed, hips rolling as she came up behind me while I turned to face her. "Remember me?"

"Uh . . . " The answer to that was no. There was something familiar about her features, I guess. And normally, being a bionic means I don't forget faces, but I didn't want to spend the millisecond it would take to search my memory banks to match her face to any one memory.

She laughed at me. "Penny, remember? We spent that crazy night together back in January during that big snowstorm?" Her bright eyes flashed as she advanced on me.

"You're not supposed to be here," I said even as she pressed against me. I stepped back to put distance between us, unenthused. "Why don't you get on out of here, huh?"

She stepped forward. "Oh, come on. You told me you love a woman who takes what she wants." She played with the lapels of my suit jacket. "I want you."

The old me, the one who never knew who Madison Hadley was, would've bent her over the sink and screwed her senseless right there before giving her a slap on the ass and sending her on her way. But nothing about that opportunity has any kind of sway over me anymore.

All I could think about was my feisty bombshell in the stands, the woman that dressed up for me, came out for me, rooted for me when she didn't have any idea what she was in for. Not a fan, not a groupie, not a one-night stand.

My girl. The only woman for me.

So I removed Penny's hands from my jacket, taking her gently but firmly by the wrists.

"You need to leave," I said, a little more sternly.

Penny pouted and pounced on me, seizing me in a kiss I didn't want. I spread my arms out to the side, processor whirling.

"I said no," I said, but she wasn't listening, still kissing me as her hands wandered. Without my inhibitor chip, I can technically defend myself, and lethally, if necessary. But after my previous close call that almost cost me my entire fighting career, I really didn't want to hurt the girl.

There was nothing even remotely sexy about the way she attached herself like a vacuum to my face, backing me up until I ran smack into a urinal. I finally shoved her from me and was seconds from twisting her arm behind her back and escorting her out by force when Madison came into the bathroom.

The projection of the video clip ends. The anger and hurt in Madison's eyes slowly fade as her expression softens into a shocked frown. She puts her phone back into her purse.

"I thought . . . "

"I know what you thought," I reply softly, resting my hands in my pockets.

She breathes out slowly. "I've never been so mad in my whole life. Holy shit."

I'm not mad at her. How can I be? I try to imagine what I'd feel like if I walked in on a guy pushing her up against a bathroom counter, smothering her face with his lips. The thought alone makes me want to rip something apart.

"Really?" I have to tease her, just a little. "I couldn't tell. Remind me to never piss you off for real."

Her expression is uncertain, like she isn't sure whether

to laugh or smile. The whole thing's shaken her, and I can't blame her.

She slings her purse over her shoulder. "I'm not a jealous person, but seeing her with you like that, I . . . "

"I like jealous."

Now that the crazy blond fan incident is behind us, I can take all the time I need to drink Madison in. Her little black dress, the legs I love on display, gorgeous brown hair down, makeup on point.

I take a step toward her. "But maybe next time kick *her* ass instead of mine."

She scoffs at me. "There's going to be a next time?" She stomps past me as though she means to do just that. "Ooh, I'll rip her heart out—"

I catch her in the crook of my arm. "Hey, hey, hey. Easy, princess. No murder tonight. You never know with this gig." I take her hand in mine and gently pull her toward me. "I'll have to talk with Ky about better security measures. How's that?"

"Better," she admits, gazing up at me as her arms slowly slide around my shoulders, much to my delight. "I think you're missing your interview."

"Nah, it's Ky's show. He can enjoy the limelight and be mad at me about it later." I pull her closer. "I've got something more important right in front of me."

Madison shakes her head and pulls away to dig in her purse.

I let her go, confused. "What? What is it?"

"You've still got your little friend's lipstick on your face." She pulls out a small makeup wipe and cleans me up until she's satisfied. "There. Erased. Never happened." She slips her arms around me again. "You still haven't asked me, you know."

"Well, I'd planned on something a little more romantic and a little less *dramatic.*" I curl my arms around her waist. "Guess I should've thought up a Plan B. We'll miss our reservations at this rate."

"Reservations?" She smiles hopefully at me. "You were gonna take me out?"

"Of course I was. A proper night on the town. A date." She's so beautiful, it's all I can do to keep from leaning down and kissing her right then and there, but near the parking garage doesn't exactly scream romance. I want the moment to be right. "I could still take you for a drive, though."

Madison's grin is infectious. "You better."

Half a century ago, all vehicles had to be driven manually. That hasn't been the case for some time now, and my ride is no exception. It's a damn good thing too. It's hard to concentrate when Madison is lounging on the passenger side seat of my car, wearing the little black number she has on. I run a quick diagnostic scan—it's cheating, I know, but my curiosity gets the best of me—and see her temperature has spiked.

That reassures me that I'm on the right track.

"So?" Madison asks, crossing her ankles with one elbow resting on the car door. She's rolled the window down, not seeming to care that the breeze tousles her hair as we fly on by.

I don't mind it, either. Makes her look wild, untamed, closer to what she really is. The more I learn about her, speak to her, know her, the more I break barriers and understand why the construct of human society is so fucking inaccurate. The idea of a concert pianist springs to mind someone stuffy, condescending, snobbish. When I first met her, that's precisely what I thought she was.

But none of that is really Madison.

I glance over at her. "So."

"Where are you taking me?" she asks.

"Vanderbilt Overlook. You can see the riverboat all lit up, the bridge, the whole works."

"Isn't that a lover's lane?"

My hands loosen on the steering wheel and let it go as I activate the fully automated driving system. "I don't know, you tell me. You've technically been around a lot longer."

"What's that supposed to mean?"

"You're the sexy older woman, Madi." I can't help but tease her; she makes it so easy for me. "I mean, technically my processor is only four years old. I'm just a little baby."

"Do *not* say that." She snorts, giggling at me.

We lock eyes as my car safely hurtles down the highway, driving us toward our destination. The way she looks at me, the yearning I see in her gaze, makes me want to cancel the drive and take her straight home.

"You are anything but a baby."

"Glad we've got that straight."

There's a reason I chose Vanderbilt Overlook as our destination. It's far enough away from the city with a beautiful view of the river and the Vanderbilt Bridge, as well as clearer, starlit skies away from all the lights.

I put the car in park and initiate a command to put the top down, then point upwards. "We're in luck. Guess there's no other lovers tonight."

She gasps as she looks up. "Dom . . . "

My processor does a little victory dance, though I can play it cool enough. "Never star-gazed before?"

"No," Madison admits, blushing just a little. "Not really, not where I could really appreciate the view. Or . . . when I was with the right guy."

Bingo. I perk up a little as I turn toward her. "I'm the right guy now?"

She gazes at me, biting her lip. "You were always the right guy."

This gorgeous woman is practically begging to be kissed, and I can't hold off anymore. She leans in, her lips parted, and I meet her halfway, my mouth eagerly colliding against hers. Electricity dances along my circuits in a way it never has before, gratification drive gone haywire.

She's the woman I was always meant to satisfy. She's it.

She is everything.

When our kiss breaks, she stares at me in a daze beneath half-lidded eyes. "Oh, Dom."

She takes hold of the collar of my shirt and pulls me in for another kiss, which I am more than happy to oblige. I've never felt this kind of dizziness before, not even while fighting earlier. The world is spinning, but in the best way.

All because of one kiss.

She's breathless as I smooth my hand over her dress.

"Do you want me to take you home?" I murmur against her lips.

Her features alight with mischief, she flips off her heels without care and crawls over the seat into the back, pulling me with her.

"What are you—" I follow, albeit somewhat clumsily. I'm a big machine; I don't crawl well over anything.

After I'm settled in the backseat, Madison sits on my lap and kisses me with a zeal I can easily match. I'm pleasantly surprised. This woman's got an appetite on her. My arms are around her waist at first, but then my hands wander.

One smooths up and down her back while the other grazes her thigh.

Emboldened, her kisses are laced with heat. I feel traces of her lipstick all over my mouth, and she trails kisses to my jaw and nibbles on my ear.

"Touch me, Dom," she whispers, sending little shocks of delighted voltage down my circuitry while I sit wide-eyed, wondering if I heard what I thought I just heard. "Please."

A slow, triumphant grin tugs at the corners of my mouth and finally spreads across my face, eyeing her as I inch my right hand up beneath her dress, fingertips brushing along the smooth, creamy skin of her inner thigh. Her panties are already damp. My touch glides along her soft mound and lightly traces her slit over the fabric, eliciting a gasp from her.

"You're teasing me . . . "

"Consider it payback," I reply, grasping her silken hair with a gentle fist, pulling her toward me. "C'mere." Our mouths collide again as I finally push aside her underwear.

I let forth a short, victorious chuckle against her lips, our kisses deep and hungry. "You're so wet."

Curling one arm around her hips, I pull her closer on my lap, pushing one finger inside her.

Her back arches, arms around me, and she moans. "Dominic!"

My name on her lips like that tempts me to lose control, but I harness my own desire and play the patient game. I start slowly at first, pumping my finger gently in and out of her until I discover a rhythm she likes. She grinds against my hand, biting her lip and whimpering, wanting more. A second digit joins the first, and she gasps, eyes half-lidded under a lusty spell.

"You've wanted this for a while, haven't you, princess?"

I muse, pulling away from her intoxicating kisses but drinking in how lost in passion she becomes, squirming in my grasp.

When I call her *princess* her breath hitches, and I feel her tensing. Her orgasm is close.

"Dom," she warns, panting.

"You like this? Getting fucked by a droid?" My thumb finds her clit, gently circling, rubbing, and flicking.

She's responsive to my voice as well as my fingers. I hoped she would be.

"Y-yes."

I pull her into another deep kiss, then my lips find her ear, nipping her earlobe as I relentlessly plunder her sex with my fingers. "Come for me, princess."

Her breathing heightens into soft, audible cries of ecstasy, my name as her thighs close, legs clenching around my arm as her first climax rocks her entire body. I briefly switch my visual feed to a heat scan, drinking in just how warm she is post-orgasm as I pry her knees apart roughly.

"Nuh uh. I'm not done."

I'm not the tallest of the bionics out there, but that doesn't change the fact that the backseat of my car wasn't exactly meant for hookups. I've avoided this setting with other dates in the past, not looking to hit my head or hers by accident and throw off the mood with any clumsy antics.

It's different with Madison, though. I maneuver her into straddling me and she squeaks when her hair catches on the metal of the driver's seat headrest.

"Wait, wait, wait—"

"Sorry." My knees strain against the front seats, and I'm too large to lie down flat. I gently pull her hair free, managing not to damage the strands caught in the process.

It doesn't bother her in the slightest, and her soft laughter rings in my ear.

"You okay?"

"It's fine."

She returns to kissing me as I slide her underwear off her hips, peeling it down her legs until she successfully kicks it off one ankle. It all seems so natural, even when things don't go as smoothly as I pictured.

I'm still trying to figure out our little size problem. I go through a dozen different scenarios, processor worrying, until I lock down on one.

I'm going to have to get creative.

Lifting Madison isn't a struggle, but she flails and holds onto my shoulders in confusion.

I gaze up at her. "I want to taste you."

She turns a deep shade of red, flustered. "H-how?"

Pulling myself out of the constraints of the backseat, I swing her legs over my shoulders and twist to set her rear down on the back of my car. Madison goes where I guide her, catching on quickly. She sets her hands down on the shiny, steel back chrome and leans back as I spread her legs wide, pushing up her dress.

The view of her soft mound, natural with little brown curls and glistening with heat, is enough to overwhelm my sensors one hundred times over. I lean in, tracing kisses up her thigh, glancing up and scanning her. She watches me in awe as her heart rate quickens. The adoration I see in her face goads me on.

My princess is pleased with me. Good.

Taking in her sweet scent, I tentatively flick my tongue along her outer folds. She gasps and moves her fingers into my hair as I continue teasing her, licking up one way and down another until I spread her lips apart and begin drinking in her pink velvet pussy.

Madison's legs jerk in response as she grips me. "Dom!"

With my tongue swirling around her clit, occasionally nibbling, I continue teasing her and don't let up, firmly holding those milky legs apart even as she squeaks and squeezes against me. Still sensitive from her last release, she squirms, moans, and grinds against my face.

"Dom, I'm going to come." I keep going, faster now, and her body tenses. "Dom, I'm coming!"

Finally, I let her legs go, and her thighs close around my head. She bites back another ecstatic cry as I eagerly lap her up, riding through her orgasm. Breathing isn't a necessary bodily function of mine, though if I were going to suffocate, I can't think of a better way to go.

Madison relaxes, and I pull her toward me. "That was . . ."

I kiss her deeply, reaching around her to unzip her dress. I've wanted to see what was beneath her clothes ever since she sashayed into my life with a chip on her shoulder. I've never celebrated my activation date, but this is the closest thing to a birthday to me.

I unwrap her slowly, taking time to memorize every freckle, every inch of her. After I unhook her bra, she pulls her straps down over her shoulders and casts it aside. Her tits are perfect. I stare at her for a moment before my kisses resume, one hand fondling her breast, her nipple peaking at my touch.

"I want to taste you now," she protests, reaching down and palming my groin.

My cock is already rock hard, trapped beneath my jeans, and a pulse of electric pleasure courses through me.

She fumbles with my pants, unzipping me, until I grasp her wrist.

"Later," I groan. I need to be inside this woman, right now.

She pouts at me. "But then you'll be finished."

"So? I don't go limp, baby. I'm fully initialized and ready to go until you decide *you're* done."

Her eyes widen considerably. Endlessly amused, I steal kisses while she processes this information.

"Wait. So you can . . . "

"Over." Kiss. "And over." Another kiss. "And over again."

"Oh my god," she murmurs, kissing me harder now. "You're amazing. You're like . . . a woman."

"Well, let's not go that far." Laughing softly, I pull her onto my lap again. Madison withdraws my cock from the fly of my pants, giving me a few strokes before straddling me and pressing my head against her lips. She aligns herself and sinks down on me until she's taken me in to the hilt.

"Oh, yes," she whispers.

A little noise in the back of her throat matches the satisfied groan I bite back. We sit there, lost in a brief, shared moment. Finally. Fucking finally. I'm bottomed out in this beautiful woman, the one I've wanted since the very beginning.

And judging by the way she's gazing into my eyes, she feels the same way.

She grinds in my lap, kissing me deeply.

"You feel so good," I reassure her between her little moans and smoldering kisses. "So good, princess." Her pussy is tight, gripping me snugly.

What starts as slow and sensual picks up speed as she rides. Each of my sensors is overwhelmed in the best way.

Her little black dress is bunched up around her hips, breasts bouncing as I grip her rear and drive into her harder, faster. The scent of her warm cashmere perfume lingers in the fresh air around us, clashing with the smell of recent rain.

Nothing is more intense than this. She has every receptor of mine wrapped around her finger. My dick pulses, my own release building. She's ravenous for me, panting desperately, breath heightening as her body begins to tense and shudder.

"Dom," she whispers. "Dom, I'm—"

When she drops her rhythm, I pick it up. "Show me how you come, Madi. I want to feel it."

I pull her into a harsh kiss and hold her tightly as I muffle her delightful cry, and finally allow myself to come with her, voltages of pleasure jolting through me. She collapses against me, and I cradle her in my arms, burying my face into her neck and pressing softer, sweeter kisses over her damp skin. When she pulls away, I cup her face, gently tracing my thumbs over her rosy cheeks.

"I think I almost passed out there," she admits with a sheepish giggle, folding her arms over her breasts as though she's suddenly shy.

I won't let her cover herself. "Can't have that." I push her arms apart, guiding them around my shoulders, instead. My clothes are disheveled. I give her one final glance over, committing every gorgeous inch of her to memory, before I reach for her bra and help her fix her gown.

"Dom?" she whispers as I carefully slip her dress straps over her arms again and zip up behind her.

I glance up at her, meeting her eyes. "Yeah?"

"Do you wanna stay with me tonight?" She brushes her lips teasingly against mine.

I perk up instantly, my processor practically dancing

across the motherboard in my head. This woman isn't *done* with me.

"What about James?"

She tilts her head, smiling coyly. "You'll just have to keep me quiet."

That's the hottest thing I've ever heard. I help her into the passenger seat and hop behind the wheel, bringing the car roof back up around us.

"Oh, fuck yes."

NEW CARNEGIE TIMES

JULY 5, 2069

LOVE TURNED COLD: INTERNATIONAL ANDROID MURDER CASE DRAWS ACU SPECIALIST AND BNP99 TO PARIS

As American android owners, especially those looking to benefit from modification, celebrate their legal win in the US, other countries are still undecided as to whether they will outlaw inhibitor chip removal.

The one exception? France.

A developing story turned sensational last year when android owner and housewife Madeleine St. Pierre was arrested and charged with the cold-blooded murder of her husband Andre. The family cyborg Jacques was also taken into custody.

Androids in France are still an uncommon luxury, as BioNex stores in France and the UK have only been open for little under two years. French officials are said to have contacted BioNex Corporation directly in order to commission their own BNP unit. In the meantime, New Carnegie Police Department sent the head of their growing Artificial Crimes Unit, Lieutenant Deion Washington, to Paris with his investigative bionic assistant Ezra to assist the French prefecture.

Post-investigation, Madeleine St. Pierre was successfully and swiftly charged in the murder of her husband, removing her android's inhibitor chip, and instructing it to kill Andre while he slept. A judge found her guilty last week and sentenced her to life in prison. Her android will be returned to BioNex Corporation and subsequently deactivated.

"It's an amazing thing, really," Washington says. "Androids record everything that happen around them at any given time. Ezra has this fantastic capability where he can override other android security measures and access their visual feeds. You can compare it to mind-reading, I guess. Then he withdraws the pertinent information, copies it, and sends it to investigators. The French police weren't expecting to see the murder occur in front of their very eyes, but there it was."

The French government was quick in the aftermath of this case to pass a law strictly forbidding any kind of tampering with android inhibitors. Violators could face hefty fines or even two years imprisonment.

[7]

Madison

The week after Dominic's winning match has been amazing.

We can't get enough of each other. I've told him I'm not ready to tell Dad quite yet, and he understood, so we try not to make it completely obvious in the daytime when taking care of Dad always takes precedence.

Dad's not an idiot, though. I'm not sure how much longer I can avoid the subject.

It's difficult. I can't take my eyes off Dominic as he works. He wasn't lying when he said it would only take him a day to set up the porch, and he teased me the entire time, working with his shirt off as he drilled the wood together. He'd occasionally glance at me and wink or smile, and despite my best efforts, I couldn't wipe the stupid grin off my face.

Because of his handiness, we saved some money on labor, and Dad finally gets what he wanted: warm, comfortable summer nights outdoors, admiring sunsets while Dominic roasts food on his coveted stainless grill.

We lounge on patio furniture with our feet up and drink beer and wine coolers until the sun goes down.

"This is what . . . " Dad says quietly to himself, looking around as he grips his beer.

I glance over at him. "What's that, Dad?"

He turns his head slowly, smiles sadly, and looks out at our backyard and the evening sky turning from bright blue to pink, orange, and crimson.

"This is what it's all about."

Then he drops his beer, and I quickly rise to grab it as golden amber liquid spills through the cracks of his new porch. He makes a noise of frustration and curses from the corner of his mouth.

"It's all right, Dad. It's just a little spill. No big deal." I offer the can to him with a smile. If I smile, he can't see how I've been jolted out of this romantic fantasy back into reality, and the guilt that comes after. "You want the rest?"

He swallows and looks at me. "No."

"Okay." I set it aside and sit back down.

As Dad goes back to enjoying the sunset, I subtly watch him. It hits me hard, and I realize it's only after Dominic's been here helping me that I see past my own stress. I've been trying to ignore my father's disease. Denying it. Inwardly telling myself I still have time.

I don't have much time left at all.

Suddenly I remember every memory I've ever shared with my dad. What it was like, riding on his shoulders. How he helped me ride my first holo-bike. My first piano recital at eight years old when he brought me roses and presented them to me in front of everybody. Bringing flowers every spring to my mother's grave. His reunions with his war friends. Seeing him proudly standing in his old uniform in front of the Ukrainian War memorial in DC on the anniversary of the ceasefire with his comrades, and how his expression crumpled when I innocently searched and found the name of his longest and greatest friend, lost in a battle he won't talk about with me.

That was the first time I ever saw him cry. The last was when he told me at my graduation that he's never been prouder of me in his life.

The inevitability of losing him never really sank in, until now.

He should be enjoying his retirement years, seeing the world, maybe finally allowing himself to move on from Mom and finding love again. Instead, I've watched him struggle to walk until he can't anymore. I've watched his feet fail him, curling unnaturally as he's been bound to his wheelchair, his muscles slowly dying, bit by bit.

It's all I can take to stop myself from bursting into tears and bawling in front of them both.

Dominic glances over his shoulder at us as he grills, his expression fading from smiling to neutral. When Dad can't hold his fork and knife steady, he helps him cut up his food, and it takes him longer than usual to feed him.

Before tonight, we made love every night. We tried once to just cuddle and hold each other when I was feeling pretty raw, but it eventually devolved into sex on the couch when I instigated. I felt like a teenager or a college kid again. It's been a long time since I behaved this way.

But Dominic senses my needs before I can even make sense of them. As we lie together in bed, I stare at the ceiling. His fingers trail over my abdomen lightly as he props himself up with his elbow. There's no trace of his infectious smile.

"Talk to me," he murmurs. "Tell me what's on your mind."

"I'm not sure I can," I whisper. "It's . . . hard to find the words."

Dominic's tone is gentle, patient. "Try."

I shut my eyes, steeling myself, and turn on my side to face him. I feel so exposed.

"I'm the strong one. I've always had to be. Everyone's always relied on me to keep everything together, even when everything's falling apart." My voice cracks. "And I'm not sure I can do it anymore."

"Hey," he says soothingly, sitting up and pulling me with him. "Come here."

I move into his lap, and he puts his arms around me. He's shirtless but so incredibly warm with his synthetic skin against mine.

I keep going. "It's not fair. Nothing about this is fair."

His hand glides across my back, rocking me. "I know."

"You don't know." I pull away to look at him. I'm not angry, I'm not lashing out. I'm just talking. For once I'm talking about it, and it's like I can't stop. The gates are open, and I can't shut them again. He pauses, so I continue.

"I don't mean that as a jab. I mean you can't know what it's like. Nobody can. This burden I've been carrying, watching him fade, pretending everything's going to be all right so his last few months aren't just miserable while my sister practically can't wait for him to die. For *money*."

"Madi." He brushes tears from my cheeks with a thumb. "It's okay to feel tired. You've run yourself ragged. You need to give yourself a break."

"I can't." My lip quivers as I meet his eyes. "He'll never walk me down the aisle, Dom. He'll never dance with me at my wedding. He'll never meet his grandkids, if I have any.

He won't . . . " It all finally crashes down. "He won't see me play at Carnegie Hall."

I can't form a coherent thought anymore. Dom presses his lips against my temple and holds me tightly, letting me cry into his shoulder until I can't anymore.

Dominic is the only aspect of my life that feels right. But happiness can only linger for so long.

On Monday morning, Dominic gets in early. He helps Dad out of bed, gets him freshened up, brings him to his wheelchair, and helps him eat breakfast. We go to the hospital together for his regular checkup. Dominic is all smiles, trying to keep Dad's spirits up, talking about sports and the game they're going to watch tonight.

But the doctor shatters our optimism.

Dad's disease has spread to his shoulders, quicker than they anticipated. They say a week, maybe two, until it reaches his neck and face.

Talking, swallowing, and even breathing will become difficult.

Then, impossible.

Hearing them say it aloud is like being lined up in front of a firing squad of medical professionals. I stare straight ahead as anger, resentment, grief, everything builds up. They talk so clinically. I see pity in their eyes, but pity isn't enough. They get to go home to their families. They're not losing anyone.

What's worse is seeing the defeat in Dad's eyes when they tell him. I've never seen him so utterly crestfallen. He's the sort of man who never surrenders. The kind who fixes things, who doesn't take no for an answer. Seeing him finally relent, finally accept he can't escape from this, is more than I can bear.

I won't cry in front of Dad, but it's hard to keep it together. On the drive home, I toy with the car's command center, which lights up and glows at my touch. Dominic is in the driver's seat, glancing at me.

"What should we listen to, Dad? Want some oldies—Bruno Mars? Michael Bublé?"

He doesn't answer. Just stares bleakly out the window.

I only want to see him smile. Just another smile, before he can't anymore.

When we get home, he's unable to use the touch holopad of his wheelchair to move it forward, and he can't tilt himself to activate its pressure sensors, either. I help him roll to the study and position him in front of the piano.

Music is all I've got. All I can control. All I can give him.

"I'll play your favorite, okay?"

I begin playing *Fountains of Villa d'Este* by Franz Liszt, the very piece I played for my piano finals at the Conservatory. I haven't touched it in ages, but I memorized it, and it all comes back to me swiftly. I can't think about mistakes now. I just play, pouring everything into it. Dominic sits next to Dad, listening and saying nothing.

After I've played, I look over at Dad. He's crying.

Startled, I rush to him. "Dad?"

"My girl." He sniffles and he presses his forehead to mine as I embrace him. "My sweet girl."

After I've settled him down, Dominic helps by making a few calls to family while I escape to my room and lock myself in the bathroom to cry my eyes out. By the time I've composed myself, I've got another problem on my hands.

Chloe, walking through my door with her husband and kids.

"Madi!" Chloe cries, as though we haven't seen each other for years, arms flung out toward me.

I hold my tongue as Chloe makes her little show of greeting me, half-heartedly returning her hug while Dominic watches.

"We came as soon as we could. Kind of you to have your android call us."

Ryleigh and Anton have already scurried downstairs to pull out every toy they can find. I shouldn't be annoyed with the children. They're just kids. They don't understand this kind of thing, but regardless, I'd rather not deal with them right now.

"Heard what?" My annoyance is masked by only a thin veil of tolerance, but Chloe has already sidled along past me and headed for the living room to drape herself on Dad.

That leaves us with Ryan as he takes off his shoes.

"Finally gave in and got a droid, huh?" He makes a point of not looking directly at Dominic, pretending like he doesn't exist, and squares his shoulders a little.

"Weak," he taunts. "And here I thought you had everything handled, Mads."

I refrain from rolling my eyes. Ryan is the quintessential macho man—beers, fishing trips, football, living his life with rules like *crying-is-for-wimps* and *I-don't-need-directions*. He's a blue-collar man turned white-collar due to Chloe's endless harassment, moving from the salary at their local firefighting department to insurance and sales.

Even so, he'd be manageable if he weren't a hundred times more annoying due to his complete lack of personality. I could have a more interesting conversation with a block of cement.

I've learned not to engage him when he baits me like that. But I forgot to give Dominic the memo.

"She does," he counters for me. "She can't lift him, and he's not comfortable undressing in front of his daughter. That's why I'm here."

"Easy, champ," Ryan says with a mocking smile. "I'm just giving her a hard time. Aren't I, Mads?"

Dominic glances at me. I'm not in the mood for jokes, but I'd rather avoid an argument. Ryan cruises past us to greet Dad as Chloe returns.

"Well, I guess there's no point in delaying it. We should talk about some things."

I frown at her. "Like?"

"Preparations, of course," Chloe says in a tone so flippantly callous and unthinking, not even bothering to lower her voice, even I'm in disbelief. "Make sure his will and everything is in order. We'll have to go through matters of his estate—"

The years of resentment and anger finally boil up.

"What the hell are you doing?" I hiss.

Chloe deflects. "Just being responsible. I know you and I haven't been as close, but we still need to—"

"He isn't dead yet." I cut through her words like I'm holding a blade, pointing every ounce of venom I can muster at my sister. "You don't get to talk about him like he is."

"Of course he isn't, but he will be soon, Madi. So we—"

"Lower your goddamn voice," I demand, fuming at her. "Dad can hear you."

"Oh." She shrugs. "Sorry, I wasn't thinking about it."

"That's the thing, isn't it?" I dig my fingernails into my palms as my entire body clenches. "You never think unless it's about money and what benefits you."

Dominic stands next to me with his arms folded, remaining silent.

Chloe feigns being wounded. "You're so cruel to me. Ever since I got married, you've been nothing but rude, closed off, jealous—"

I scoff. "I'm not jealous of you. You are a self-absorbed, useless, greedy bitch, and I hate that we're related."

"Madi," Dominic murmurs, urging caution.

I've raised my voice without realizing. Dad can definitely hear us now.

Unfortunately, so can Ryan.

"The fuck did you say to her?" Ryan comes storming down the corridor back into the foyer, his ire directed at me, fists clenched. "Madison, I've put up with your attitude a long time, but if you don't fucking shut your mouth—"

I back away from him as Chloe smiles at me triumphantly, reassured by her beer-gutted knight in shining armor. But her smile doesn't last.

Dominic steps between me and Ryan. "You'll what?"

"She could use a good slapping around with how her mouth pops off." Ryan's bristling, squaring up, and I can see what's about to happen before it even begins. "Get out of the way, Tin Man."

I've lost control of the situation, and I don't know what to do. "Dominic, don't—"

"Move," Ryan orders.

"No," Dominic replies, feet planted firmly apart.

Then Ryan takes a swipe at his head.

Dominic dodges. "Don't do this," he warns. "Come at me again, and I'll put you down."

"You fucking tin can piece of shi—" Ryan tries to strike him again.

I watch helplessly as it all transpires. There's no return from this.

It doesn't last long. Maybe Ryan's won a scrap or two, but Dominic can read his every movement like it's textbook. He weaves, avoiding the strike, and when Ryan charges at him, Dominic steps out of the way, grabs him, and slams him into the floor.

Chloe shrieks as her husband is locked in a wrestling hold with Dominic's arm wrapped around his neck, the other holding him fast so he can't flail or wriggle out of it.

Ryan's facc turns red then purple from lack of oxygen.

Chloe fumbles with her phone, her voice a higher octave. "I'm calling the police!"

Her children have returned to the top of the basement stairs, watching in partial amazement and horror.

I find my feet, rush toward the men, and grab Dominic's shirt. "Dom, let him go. Please. Let him go."

Dominic gives him a final squeeze for good measure before he drops Ryan to the floor and pushes him off. Ryan gasps for breath as color returns to his face. Chloe leans over him and fans him as she cries.

She turns on me like a frightened cat, pointing a perfectly manicured nail at Dominic. "That—*thing*—is going to be incinerated. I'm going to press charges. I'm going to sue!"

There's a glee to her hysteria, like somehow this has just solved all of her problems.

My heart sinks down into my gut.

She collects her children and her husband, whose only true wound was to his pride. She slams the door so hard, the chandelier above the entry shakes.

In the living room, my dad calls weakly, "Please don't fight. Please."

His voice snaps me back into reality as Dominic and I rush into the living room and find him in tears where we left him, and I kick myself a thousand times over.

"I'm sorry you heard that, Dad." I embrace him and kiss his forehead. "It's going to be okay. Sisters fight sometimes."

It's a lie, but one I feel like I have to tell him. Chloe and I have been strained for years. I know an outburst like that was bound to happen sooner or later, but I tried. I really tried to postpone it until after Dad was gone, so he wouldn't have to hear it. I always knew it would hurt him.

Immeasurable guilt clouds my swimming thoughts. The gratification the altercation brought me, like the scuffle itself, is too brief. Dominic stays back as I calm my father and finally pull away, moving toward him.

"It was a mistake. I'm sorry," he murmurs. "Should've just let him hit me. Not like it would've hurt, anyway."

Blaming Dominic is furthest from my mind. He's been pushed around, sneered at, and whatever else for God only knows how long. He shouldn't have to put up with it. He's a fighter. He always has been.

Oh God. What have I done?

"It wasn't you. It was me. I went there. I shouldn't have." I squeeze tightly when I feel his arms wrap around me, no longer caring if Dad sees. In the corner of my eyes, I see him watching us.

"You should go back," Dad urges. "You should hurry."

"No," Resigned, Dominic goes to him and gently pats his shoulder. "Not this time, Sergeant." Trying to lighten the mood with his infectious smile, he winks at me. "Whatever happens, happens. I'm tired of hunkering down, hiding like I'm a criminal."

His devil-may-care attitude does little to soothe my worry. "Dominic, what if they—"

"If they do, we'll deal with it," Dominic replies. "I'm staying."

What little optimism we have doesn't pan out. Chloe was in the car as she called the police, and Ryan didn't have a chance to lick his wounds, let alone stop her. She's been sending me wall after wall of texts, smug and self-righteous. I hate that I can't even justify myself. I was the one to start the fight, and though Dominic finished it on my behalf, it could cost us everything.

I'm going to sue you for every penny. The last small novel she texted me finishes with that single sentence. ***You'll be so broke, you'll be living in a box.***

Some sister.

Within the hour, there's a loud knock; forceful, incapable of being missed or ignored. Dominic turns off the water and wipes his hands as he finishes the dishes while I walk to the front door, my heart in my throat. He comes up behind me.

"It's all right, Madi," he says soothingly.

I want to believe him, but I'm not sure I can.

I slowly open the door before there's a second knock and stare up into the stoic features of two officers dressed in street clothes. One looks to be in his prime, umber-skinned and a little grizzled, with some salt in his peppery hair and goatee. Any warmth and compassion he has are guarded and secure beneath a dark, penetrating gaze.

I don't think I could lie to this man even if I wanted to. He'd know.

"Miss Hadley?"

"Yes," I answer quickly, looking at the other man and

freezing. The old phrase "tall, dark, and handsome" comes to mind, but it's his stark white pupils that get me. He's an android.

His narrow gaze finds Dominic. "You."

Dominic shoves his hands in his pockets. "Ezra. Long time, no see."

"You know this one?" The other officer looks between them quizzically.

"Yes. You don't remember this jackass?" Ezra says flatly, staring down Dominic as though he means to shrink him with his glare.

"I remember you sounding British," Dominic counters quickly. "Whole foreign charm thing wasn't working out for you, huh?"

Ezra's cold stare turns toward me. "*You* own him? Since when?"

"Hey," Dominic says, tone turning irate. "You can ask me the questions. I'm the one who did it. She don't *own* me. Nobody does."

"That's bullshit, and you know it. Who?"

There's a tense moment of silence, then Dominic relents in annoyance. "Kyrone Johnson. Same as last time. I'm here helping her with her father. He's got ALS."

"Last time?" Bewildered, I look at Dominic.

He shakes his head at me. "Little boxing party got broken up by this killjoy. It's no big deal."

"All right, that's enough," the other man says. Utterly confused, I turn to him. "Detective Deion Washington with the Artificial Crimes Unit. Call came in that your android assaulted a man."

Wilting like a flower isn't in my nature, and I won't tremble in front of him.

"It was in self-defense," I reply. "My sister's husband

came at me. Dominic tried to warn him. He swung anyway."

"Dominic?" Washington repeats. "As in, the winner from the fight a couple weeks back?"

"That's me." Dominic folds his arms smugly. "No autographs, please."

"There won't be any fans where you're going." Ezra isn't impressed, the edge in his voice flat and heavy. "Did you assault an organic?"

"Assault sounds a little aggressive. I was defending someone." Dominic glares back at him. "She's telling the truth. Guy came at her. I got in the way."

Washington and Ezra exchange looks. He nods. "Go ahead."

Ezra removes a pair of strange cuffs from his utility vest that he wears over his plainclothes. They're not made of steel but of some kind of smooth, white material I've never seen before.

Dominic apparently hasn't seen them before, either. He seems almost amused by them. "You know those aren't going to do anything, right? I'm just saying, I could break right through—"

Gasping and nearly tripping backwards, I put space between myself and Ezra after he launches forward and slams Dominic against the wall, pressing two of his fingertips against Dominic's temple.

Dominic freezes, stiff as a board, and then his head slowly lowers, the white of his eyes going dull as he powers down and stares at nothing.

Barely holding back angry tears, I glare at Ezra. "What did you do to him?" I demand, voice rising.

The bionic investigator ignores my outburst, situating Dominic's still body as he likes.

"Calm down," Washington interjects firmly before I can say anything more. "We're going to take him into the precinct, Ezra is going to review his story, and we'll go from there."

A twinge of hope pulls at me. "So you'll see he's telling the truth?"

"Probably. Bots don't *typically* lie," Washington replies as Ezra carries Dominic toward their car and unceremoniously stuffs him into the backseat. He's hardly the gentle sort. "But I'm going to be frank with you, ma'am. Assault is assault. Doesn't matter if it's self-defense or not. Not when it comes to droids."

"What do you mean?"

"Let me put it this way." Washington gazes at me levelly. "When a child kicks a dog, and the dog attacks the child, what happens to the dog?"

Horrified, my lip quivers, fighting back tears. "But—"

Washington stops me. "They have no rights, Miss Hadley. None at all. You understand that?"

The silence between us threatens to unbalance me. My sister shrieked and swore and cried whenever she felt like it, while I always suffered my anger, frustrations, and hopelessness in silence. I want nothing more than to fall apart right now and beg this man to let Dominic go.

"Please."

"Let me take your phone number down," Washington says. "I'll be in touch."

NEW CARNEGIE TIMES

JULY 6, 2069

"THE ENEMY OF MY ENEMY IS MY FRIEND": NEW PUREEARTH MOVEMENT BRINGS OPPOSITION TOGETHER

In a stunning live online interview, two colorful personalities came together in person to discuss an unsettling trend growing in popularity in the internet's darkest corners: Robert Carson, founder of Humanity First, and Rebecca Schroeder, professed Pro-Bionic and City Council candidate.

The setting and atmosphere were informal as Carson and Schroeder sat down together on a sofa, appearing relaxed after shaking hands and greeting each other politely.

"I'm going to admit that I never imagined actually agreeing to this meeting," Carson said.

"And I'm going to admit I never imagined you actually accepting it," Schroeder replied. "So we're on the same page already, see?"

New Carnegie Times reporter Amber Rivera posed many questions to the unlikely pair. "First, I'd like to hear your own personal definitions of both of the groups you identify with."

"Well, I founded Humanity First, and our values are fairly

straightforward, regardless of what you might have heard in the media," Carson said. "We are pro-human, first and foremost. We dislike the term 'organic'—we're human, that's that. Our concerns are primarily big money. These oligarchs are hellbent on robbing average American citizens of their inalienable rights —life, liberty and the pursuit of happiness—by replacing their entire workforces with artificial intelligence."

"So you are anti-android?"

"I am, unapologetically," Carson said. "It's not hatred or resentment. It's simply my opinion that they have no place in the American lifestyle. They harm humanity. They make us lazy, complacent. We should always push to be the best version of ourselves, not relying on machines to do our work for us, but that's not really why I agreed to come here. The reason I agreed to come here is because I want to discuss this new group that's popping up in the UK and in the bigger cities in the US, even here in New Carnegie, and to make certain that the American public understands that we are not them."

"TerraPura," said Schroeder.

When asked by Rivera what it means to identify as a Pro-Bionic, Schroeder said, "To be Pro-Bionic is to accept having an android in one's life as an equal. We never stop seeing them as machines, per se; we recognize they are not human, but we see them as individuals, as an extension or a mirror of humanity, rather than a falsehood. To be fair, I'm not the founder. Lucy Warren is the one who coined the phrase. Ultimately, we believe we can be the best versions of ourselves alongside androids. If they are capable of adaptation, clearly we cannot grow stagnant, either."

"Can you tell me how the so-called 'Pro-Bionics' feel about the TerraPura or 'PureEarth' movement?" Rivera asked.

Carson said, "Well, I think it's important to first define what PureEarth is. And PureEarth is a disease."

"I agree with Mr. Carson. How is anyone supposed to feel about terrorists?" Schroeder said. "That's really what they are. They aren't Pro-Bionic because Pro-Bionic people want to find that balance. They also value organic humanity. Sorry," she added to Carson, who shook his head. "PureEarth wants to wipe humankind out of the equation. They made that clear with the protest bombing a few months ago."

The Humanity First bombing ultimately claimed the lives of 10 people, with 21 injured. Both the UK and the US have labeled TerraPura as an ecoterrorist group but finding the root source of the group has proven difficult for law enforcement.

Schroeder continued, "What's most disturbing is they're trying to appeal to troubled minds and impressionable youth."

Carson agreed. "They're a cult. That's what cults do—seek out the weakest and most vulnerable among us, corrupt them, and empower them to do things they wouldn't otherwise think about doing."

"They've stated they essentially want robot overlords," Schroeder said. "It's ridiculous."

"Worse," Carson said, "they don't only want overlords; they want conquerors, they want decimators, mass murders. I hate throwing this word around because it's used too often in sensationalism, and it undermines what truly happened in the Second World War, but this is the one time it fits. They want a human holocaust. They want to kill every man, woman, and child on the face of the planet so that the earth can heal from global warming, over-fishing, land development, everything. It's pro-android in the most disturbing way. And as much as I disagree with Mrs. Schroeder on her ideals, and even my old friend Algrove, this is not what androids were meant for."

"The road to hell?" Schroeder offered.

"Absolutely."

[8]

Dominic

"Wake up."

I power up with a jolt, my high-definition visual feeds coming online and blinking as most of my drives, banks, and processes are loaded. It's a disorienting sensation, kind of like riding a rollercoaster that comes to a screeching halt with a final lurching slam. I'm not groggy or sluggish as my systems resume upon command—*wait, whose command? The hell?*—but I have no idea where I am at first or how I got there. My optics whir as I try to make sense of what's happened. Everything occurred so quickly.

I'm sitting in a chair in an interrogation room. Leaning against the door is Detective Washington with his arms folded, his gaze intent on me.

This isn't good. I've had my run-ins with the ACU before. At one of my best fights before BFL started going legitimate, this fucking dynamic duo all but busted the door down and ransacked the whole place with their squad.

Apparently, a couple of Kyrone's rivals had some inappropriate dealings with some whack-ass group of android-worshippers called Terra-something. Almost got myself booked then.

And that was the first time. I dealt with Ezra again when a couple Humanity First kids decided to take a few swings at me and Monty and got more than they bargained for. We hauled ass out of there, of course, but that didn't stop the little snitches from ratting us out. Like we were the aggressors. Thankfully, Detective Washington and Ky have a bit of an understanding, and they didn't drag me out of there. Ky's even worked on some of Ezra's repairs before. We got a stern warning to stay out of trouble. A slap on the wrist.

Kyrone chewed me out plenty, and I promised to be a saint.

So much for that plan.

I try to move my arms, but I can't. They're dead weight. That same pair of odd white cuffs are secured around my wrists. They glow blue and thrum. I glance down at my legs as I try to get up, but they're similarly anchored with matching cuffs around my ankles.

"The fuck is this?" I demand, finally focusing on Ezra. He sits across the table from me, staring me down. "Why can't I move? What the fuck did you do to—"

"Calm down," Ezra commands. "I powered you down and restrained your mobility circuits. Can't have you busting down the door, can we?"

Something different, uncomfortable, pulses through my sensors. My biocomponents are cold from being powered down for some time, contributing to whatever this is I'm feeling. I've lost three hours.

I don't like this. I want out. "Where's Madison?"

"Miss Hadley isn't here," Washington replies.

"You guys must feel like you're really hot stuff, huh?" I'm indignant, even angry, at being treated this way. "Jumping a guy when he's not expecting it."

"You threatened to break your cuffs," Ezra replies simply.

"I was just saying that. I wasn't actually going to," I retort. "I would've come quietly."

"I don't think quiet is something you know how to be." Ezra rolls up his sleeves and reaches for me.

I can sense an odd kind of heat emanating from his fingertips as he moves to clasp the side of my head. Due to my binds, I can't pull away.

"What's that? What are you doing?"

Ezra doesn't answer. When his hands rest against my temples, the shutters built into my irises suddenly forcibly dilate, and his similarly widen and narrow as we signal each other. It makes a slight sound. Almost like Morse code meets vintage cameras.

He bypasses my security systems, forcing me to communicate my model and serial numbers. He unlocks my memory banks without needing so much as a password, retrieving the video feeds and going through them faster than a human being could hope to keep up with.

Within moments, he transfers the footage of my fight with Ryan to his own databanks and uploads them to his unit's servers. I hear the little *ding* from Washington's digital tablet as he pulls it out and places it on the table. With a flick of his wrist, Washington starts up the replay of what happened to review my altercation with Ryan. I can't read his reactions. Ezra still stares at me, holding my head.

"You know, if you want to kiss me," I taunt, "you could just do it."

Ezra scowls and goes through the rest of my memory banks. Panic grips my system. My ivory bio-blood is warm and toasty now.

"Hey. That's private. You have no right—"

"Shut up."

Cool and unfeeling, Ezra continues going through everything, breezing right through each and every one of my more personal memories—including every carnal, naked moment I've spent with Madison—right through my major televised fight and time spent with James.

Then he slows. He homes in on the night outside the gas station.

The night where I thrashed those anti-android thugs coming after me and Madison.

It's about right then I know I'm in deeper trouble than I bargained for. All that nobility I felt in the moments leading up to my arrest—if that's what it can be called—feels small and insignificant now. I second-guess everything. I should have called Kyrone, gotten out of there. Done something, some form of self-preservation.

If keeping Ryan in a chokehold isn't my death sentence, the damage I did to those assholes will be.

But Ezra doesn't transfer that footage.

He erases it.

We share a look as Ezra withdraws his hands and rolls his sleeves back down. I can finally look past him at Washington, who views my footage with an expression of stone.

"Well?" he asks. "Is he who you thought he might be?"

"No," Ezra responds neutrally.

I stare at him slightly slack-jawed. *Why is he lying?*

This guy knocked me the fuck out and dragged me to this place, away from the people I care about. Why the fuck is he protecting me?

"Well, this is bad news." Washington powers down the tablet and looks at me while Ezra stands behind him. "Sorry, Dom. That was an impressive show you gave at the fight. But this is damning. So long as Chloe Fischer insists on pressing charges against her sister . . . "

"I'm dead, right?"

"Permanently deactivated," Washington says somberly, shifting in the seat across from me. "That's what BioNex likes to call it."

"Dead," I repeat, gazing at him levelly.

He nods a little, finally assenting. "Dead."

"So what're you going to do with me now?"

"Are you a flight risk?" Washington asks.

It might seem an odd question, but I get it. I could probably bash through a wall and walk out of here if I had half a processor to do it. Ezra shows no sign of anything, just watches me. I still can't figure out a good reason why he deleted the most damning evidence of all directly from my visual drive. The knowledge of it remains. I know that I did it. I just can't see it anymore.

"No," I say finally. "I'm no coward. I'll stay."

"I thought not." Washington rises.

Ezra moves closer to me, raising his hand as though he means to power me down again. I don't know how he can do that with just a touch, but I tilt my head away.

"I'd like to stay awake, if I'm gonna get snuffed out," I declare. "If it's all the same to you."

Ezra looks at Washington, who nods.

"Put him in with the other prisoners. Who knows?" He says. "Maybe he can scare some sense into the other loudmouths."

I thought Washington was kidding about shutting up some wise guys. He wasn't.

After removing my mobility restraints, I'm moved into the holding cell at the police precinct, where drunkards and other small-time violators are kept overnight. In older times, that meant iron bars. Now it means a soft blue holo-energy field that looks a lot more comforting than it actually is. One touch gives you a damn good zap; not enough to kill but enough to wake someone the fuck up, and I'm not interested in frying my circuits.

Ezra throws me in for a few hours, and it only takes the prisoners a little time to figure out I'm bionic. I get a lot of mockery at first. *Garbage can, tin can, white eyes.* Normally I'd be mouthy right back, but my only thoughts revolve around Madison and James. All of my processes have slowed a bit. I don't want to be here.

I want to be there. I need to be there. With him. With her.

My silence only emboldens the other jailbirds. The altercation that follows is like the one with Ryan. Short and rather anti-climactic.

One of them gets brave and tries to come at me, and I slam him into the restriction field. He yowls and scurries away into the corner, nursing a bruised ego, hairs on every part of his body standing on end.

"Anyone else?" Resigned, weary of all this showboating, I glower as the rest of them shuffle to the other side of the cell, eyeing me warily. "Thought so."

After that I'm moved to my own cell, where I sit alone for days. They won't transport me to county because I'm not a person. Not by their standards, anyway. So I'm stuck in limbo with nothing to do but stare at the floor, the ceiling, and the sheer energy walls around me. I can't even connect to try to get a message out to Madison. They're using some sort of device to block tower signals.

Then a guard opens my door. "Someone here to see you. Come on."

Oddly enough, the guard doesn't cuff me when I expect him to. Instead, I'm brought without restraint into the same interrogation room and left alone. A few minutes later, the door opens, and it's Washington.

He nods somberly at me then steps aside as Madison comes catapulting toward me.

"Dom!"

"Madi." I catch her in my arms in shock and hold her tightly to me.

"I can only give you ten minutes," Washington says, and he actually does sound apologetic. "Make it fast."

When we're alone, my lips collide with hers, and I brush her tears away gently.

"I'm sorry I couldn't come sooner," she whispers, gazing into my eyes. "I had to get a hold of Kyrone."

"Where's James?"

"Ky sent Montavious over. He's been helping Dad while I try to figure this out." Madison traces my face, kissing me again. "It's a nightmare. I miss you. Dad misses you too."

I don't want to think about that. The seconds are ticking on by, and I'm just trying to memorize every facet of her—her look, her smell, the way she feels in my arms. Everything.

"How is he?"

Madison's strong facade is gone. Here with me, she's real and as raw as ever. Her skin is pale and there are dark circles under her red eyes. It breaks my resolve, seeing her cry. My gratification drive is all but berating me for getting myself into this mess as she continues.

"It's not good. Every day he gets worse—and with Chloe insisting on pressing charges—"

"It's going to be fine." I run my fingers through her hair. "You're strong. You're smart. You've got this. I know you do."

"Why do they have to keep you here?" Madison frowns. "I wish they could just release you to me. You're not a danger."

"That's not how it works, babe. You know that."

She rests her forehead against mine for a moment before embracing me again. I bury my face into her hair, breathing her in. She's wearing the yellow sundress—my favorite.

"You're cruel, coming in here looking this good, showing off your legs. If I was organic, I'd be blue-balled."

She snickers into my shoulder despite our circumstances. "Guess it's a good thing you can't be."

"Down there, no." I tap my temple. "Up here, maybe."

Madison takes my hands, and I press kisses against her knuckles.

"I'm going to fight her. She can't do this to you. You're not a thing. You're Dominic. I won't let her."

The determination I see despite the circles under her eyes and the weariness in her face almost makes me believe.

Almost.

I put up the strong front, anyway. I don't have the heart to tell her. Washington's already made it clear.

It's over for me.

"I believe you," I tell her half-heartedly, pressing

another kiss to her forehead as Washington comes to retrieve her. The minutes have gone by too quickly.

Reluctantly letting her go, I watch as she backs away. She doesn't turn and flee or leave right away. She stands to the side after asking Washington's permission. Our eyes meet as I'm led past her.

Then I'm back in my cell, and she's gone.

The order comes two days later.

"Your termination is scheduled."

Ezra speaks to me through the restriction field. Hearing Madison's determination before, I let myself consider that maybe, just maybe, I'd be getting out of here. Kyrone even stopped by the day before, though I only got five minutes with him. He told me he was looking over every avenue, that he'd even release the video footage to social media and get positive attention on me that way.

My life isn't just on the line. My life is forfeit right now.

"For when?" I sound calmer than I feel, hands in my pockets. It's the only stance I can take to keep myself from pacing back and forth in front of the bionic investigator like a caged animal.

"Tonight," Ezra replies.

My processors instantly flit to Madison. James. "Do I get to make a call?"

Ezra stares back at me calmly. "No."

So that's it, then. I'm to be deactivated permanently—terminated. Well, I'll call it what it is: executed. No opportunity to say goodbye to Madison, her father, Kyrone, or the guys. Anyone. I am completely isolated, except for the stoic droid in front of me.

"Answer me this, then. Why'd you do it?"

Ezra regards me silently for a moment. "Do what?"

"You know what," I counter, impatient. I don't have time to waste playing games with him.

He speaks to me as though I'm an infant. "What is my directive, Dominic?"

Fuck it. I throw up my hands. This asshole *makes* me pace. He annoys me just as much now as he did when he first burst through the door during a fight-night bust.

"I dunno, Detective Dumbass, why don't you tell me?"

"To uphold the law," he replies, appearing just as irritated with me. "Protect and serve." He looks away. "That doesn't mean I *agree*. And sometimes things aren't black and white."

I try to make sense of what he's telling me before swiftly giving up on the conversation entirely.

"I don't get you, but whatever. Thanks, I guess. I think. I don't know."

Ezra shakes his head. "I'll be back to retrieve you later."

When the time comes, Washington, Ezra, and two other officers come to fetch me. One of them enters a code on a nearby control panel that disables my cell's restriction field.

"You going to cause trouble?" The one addressing me wears patrol gear with a name strip identifying him only as Weaver.

I won't pretend like I haven't thought of escape. Beating them all senseless and making a break for it, grabbing Madison and James and running off to some paradise island somewhere no one will find us. All fantasy. They're all armed. The tasers they have on hand can do more damage to me with one deployment than their bullets, but I'm not keen on being on the opposite side of either.

Death, one way or another.

Defeat isn't in me. Every ounce of my consciousness tells me to lash out, fight back, defend myself here and now, since no one else will. Giving up isn't something I'm programmed to even consider. But neither is fear, and I feel that coursing along my circuitry, so palpable there's a foreign, metallic taste in my mouth.

Here it is. The only ring I've ever stepped into where I can't win. Every scenario is a loss that will hurt someone. James can't run off to an island paradise. He needs medical care. Madison can't abandon her dreams to live with me as a fugitive.

I have no options. No rights. No alternative.

"No," I say at last, silently wondering if this is how helpless James feels right now, and wishing I was with him and Madison back in Rockefeller Park.

There's no dreadful, deep dark room I'm taken to or an execution chamber of any kind. Instead, flanked by officers, I'm escorted off the premises to a parking lot, where a large BioNex vehicle idles far away from the others. A pair of young men waits there, wearing the uniforms of junior bionic engineers. They open the back doors at our approach.

"So that's it, then," I say aloud, no longer caring to keep my thoughts internal. I'm going to die anyway. Might as well say my piece. "You're going to put me down in the back of a van. Like I'm a stray dog."

Washington, to his credit, sounds unhappy with the decision. "I'm sorry it came to this, Dominic."

We halt as the junior engineers come to greet him.

"Evening," says one engineer to Washington. "This him?"

"Yep, this is him," Washington replies.

"Wow. The BFL's first champ," the other engineer remarks. "That was an amazing fight."

The other seems almost excited by the prospect of meeting me, his voice eager. "I won so much money off that fight. You really came through."

Ezra's eyes flash with ire as he glances at Washington, who shakes his head in disbelief. I refuse to answer until it dawns on them.

I don't have to speak a word. The others speak for me.

"You're about to shut this guy down," an officer to my left pipes up with clear distaste. "And you're fanboying. Un-fucking-believable."

"Jesus Christ, I hate this," says the officer closest to Washington. "Can we all agree this is a load of bullshit?"

"Can we get this over with, please?" says another. "My shift's done in twenty."

They fasten me to a portal activation cylinder, one smoothly lowered by their vehicle automatically by a sleek, metallic bionic lift, not unlike how Madi's van can load up James's wheelchair without issue.

"Don't worry," says one of the engineers as he powers up a tablet. "You won't feel a thing."

"*Wait!*"

Everyone turns just as the cylinder whirls to life beneath my feet, glowing bright white. Kyrone sprints toward us, followed by Madison. The engineer's finger hovers over a memory wipe command.

Breathless and hobbling on a shoe broken halfway through the heel, Madison holds up her phone, alight with a video display showing Chloe.

Madison fights to keep her hand steady, a look of mild panic plastered across her face as she speaks.

"Please, don't deactivate him."

Washington's face contorts into an expression of incredulous irritation. "What the hell is going on?"

Chloe practically shouts at him. "We're dropping all charges!"

NEW CARNEGIE TIMES

JULY 9, 2069

US ARMY ORDERS 12 BIONICS FOR FIRST FULLY ARTIFICIAL SQUAD

The Secretary of Defense announced in a press conference this evening that the US military will begin incorporating bionic soldiers into each military branch, beginning with the Army.

This announcement comes on the 30th anniversary of the final defeat of encroaching Russian forces with a stunning allied victory in the Ukraine War (2025-2040).

"We have high hopes for this partnership," says Defense Secretary Vera Dolor. "We believe this decision is best for US interests, as well as within the best interest of our fighting men and women. If we can spare even one soldier's life by sending in a perfectly trained team of androids who do not know fear, who do not know failure, then we have done the right thing."

A survey taken among active-duty military, however, shows that only 35% agree with the White House's decision, with 61% against and 4% unsure.

"They already pushed out a bunch of workers from the

private sector," says Cpl. Darrell Manning, 20, from New York. "Now they're gonna come and push us out too?"

"Everyone loves to say 'land of the free because of the brave,'" says Sgt. Eddie Stark, 32, of Alabama. "Well, it ain't brave if you can't feel nothin'. War ain't supposed to be safe. It ain't supposed to be pretty and all wrapped up in a box. If you use too many machines, you lose the ability to make humane decisions in an already inhumane situation."

Second Lt. Mariana Vasquez agrees. "Put a bunch of souped-up robots with machine guns in a situation where civilians lives might be at stake, they might make the wrong decision. A human squad is going to try and preserve human life where they can."

"I think it's great," says Pvt. Hailey Brown. "Less bullets flying at me while I'm doing my job, the better."

Recent surveys show the general public is favorable towards introducing artificial intelligence into the military, while Ukraine veterans are almost unanimously against it. The Department of Defense has been close-lipped about exactly how, when, and where this new android team would be utilized, but have shared they expect these new bionics to be fully operational by fall next year.

"We are honored to provide support to our Armed Forces," BioNex representatives said when reached for comment.

[9]

Madison

It's all so sudden.

Chloe calls me out of the blue, saying she's going to drop all charges against me and Dominic—that she's even fired her lawyer in a show of good faith.

It was her high-powered lawyers who stopped Kyrone from going to the media. They threatened him with everything under the sun. He called me not long after I texted him that they took Dominic away.

He sent Montavious over immediately to help with James when I didn't even ask him. And then he went to work. He cares about his androids; that much is certain. But they slapped a leash on him to the point where he hired a lawyer himself. We've been keeping in almost daily contact.

We're not going to lose him. He messaged me earlier that morning, when news of Dominic's termination date sent me reeling into a teary panic that left me a collapsed mess on the floor. ***I promise***.

Chloe sounds irate, and I wonder if it was Ryan twisting her arm, tired of the embarrassment of the situation or unwilling to pay the lawyer fees. I know they're in over their heads financially—buying a house they can't afford, fancy cars with massive loans they don't need, living in the fast lane when they don't have the means to do it comfortably.

"I'm going to call the precinct and tell them to release him," she tells me curtly, then disconnects.

I rush into the master bedroom where Dad is propped up with lots of pillows, watched over by Montavious. The android turns curiously when I come in, unable to contain my joy.

"Dad, she's dropping the charges. They're going to free him." I'm crying happy tears.

Montavious practically bounces over to me, excited. "Are you serious? That's—" He's so eager he runs out of the room, and then doubles back, white eyes wide. "I'm going to call Ky!" Then he runs out again.

I embrace my father, who smiles wearily at me. "I knew she would." His speech slurs.

"How did you know?"

Dad responds slowly, with care. "Because I spoke to *my* lawyer today."

"What?" I pull away and sit down next to him.

"If she went through with it, if Dom was killed," Dad says softly. He can only talk out of one side of his mouth now, and it takes him a while to get longer words out. "Her family would be written out of my will. And you would get everything."

I'm too stunned to speak, staring at him in awe, adoration, and disbelief. "You would do that?"

"She was wrong," Dad replies, having trouble swallowing as he looks away. "You go get him now. Go get him, and all will be well."

My phone vibrates in my hand. I quickly pick up. It's Chloe.

"I can't get through to them at the precinct," she says urgently.

I'm already on my feet and out the door.

"We're dropping all charges!" Chloe shouts, sounding as panicked as I feel at the sight of the engineer's hand hovering over the tablet display, moments from erasing Dominic's memory as he's mounted on a deactivation machine.

I called Kyrone as I drove like a woman possessed, unsure which of us would reach the precinct sooner. We made it just in time. I'm sick to my stomach.

Any later, and Dominic would be gone.

"Jesus Christ," Washington mutters, motioning to Ezra. "Get him off there."

The termination team looks utterly confused. "But this model jeopardizes the safety of the general public—"

Ezra glares at him, loosening the binds holding Dominic as the engineer clamps his mouth shut. He powers down the tablet, and the thundering in my chest eases. Chloe finally signs off the video, and I shove my phone into my pocket.

Dominic springs free of his restraints and crosses the parking lot to me, arms open. Our bodies collide, and we embrace each other as tightly as we can. He buries his face in the crook of my neck and hoists me into the air.

One of the officers whistles at us, as though to cheer us on, but I don't pay him any mind.

"You're safe." I cling to him tightly. "You're safe now."

"And here I'm supposed to protect you." Dominic pulls away to gaze down at me, cupping my face.

"We protect each other," I correct softly, searching his eyes. "I'm always in your corner, Dom."

His kiss collides against my mouth, claiming my lips with zeal.

"All right," Washington says. "Let's go home. Ezra, come on."

The police disperse as the BioNex van doors are shut. Within moments, it slowly drives away, the last reminder of our close call.

Kyrone's been shooting off messages on his phone left and right, no doubt informing his entire team and his wife of our victory. He claps Dominic's back.

"You are one lucky bastard. No more close calls like that. You scared the living shit out of me. Take a few weeks off. Come next season, I got a fight lined up for you, and a few rookies I need you to train in."

Dominic's arms remain around me. "Sure thing, boss. Say hello to Briyanna for me."

Kyrone snorts. "Say hello yourself. Get outta here."

Once we're alone, Dominic scoops me up into his arms like a bride.

"All right, sweetheart, let's get you home."

I laugh, my heart so full I can barely form a coherent thought beyond my own relief. *He's alive. He's safe. He's free.* I do the only thing that makes sense and steal as many kisses as he'll allow me to, which seems to be quite a few. When he's satisfied, he sets me down on my feet, and takes my car activator from me when I pull it out.

"Hey, hey, hey. Where do you think you're going with this? I'm driving." He opens the passenger side door for me.

I slide into the car. "Such a gentleman."

Dominic smirks. "Only sometimes, princess."

When we return to the house, Montavious is quick to greet Dominic.

"I'm glad they let you go, Dom. For a minute, I was scared. For all of us."

"I'm fine. Don't worry about it." Dominic claps his shoulder. "We've got a couple of allies with a badge—they weren't happy about terminating me. One in particular seems to understand."

"What do you mean?" Montavious asks.

Dominic shakes his head, ascending the stairs with me. "I'll talk to Kyrone about it later. You head home. I'll see you later." He squeezes my hand, turning his attention to me again. "How's James?"

"Not well," I admit, and all the joy and relief I feel having Dominic back with me are muted at the mention, like a world in color turning gray. "He deteriorated fast after all this."

I've already explained to him how it was Dad, not me, who finally got to Chloe. That only the threat of being left without a single penny of Dad's inheritance spared Dominic's life.

Money is what makes the world go round, including my sister, and I'm sick to death of it.

Dad is still sitting upright in his bed, resting his eyes. His lower body is tucked beneath cotton striped sheets and smooth summer blankets.

Dominic slows when he sees him, but then picks up the pace with a big broad smile.

"Who said you could sleep on the job, old timer?"

Dad's eyes open instantly, and he gives his friend a half smile, eyes shining with tears.

"Dom," he says happily. "Dom. You're home."

My heart wrenches at hearing my dad's voice like that. Weaker, almost a childlike whisper.

"Course I'm home." Dominic sits beside him, taking his hand. Dad can't feel or move his hands on his own anymore, but he can still see.

"Could never leave you and Madison for very long. You kidding me?" he says. "Montavious take care of you while I was gone? Not trying to replace me, are you?"

My father's lips quiver. His joy and triumph are trapped in his body with him, and he can only express so much. "He's a good man."

"He is," Dominic agrees. "Gonna get you up nice and early for a big pancake breakfast tomorrow. How does that sound?"

Dad watches him a moment, then his eyes meet mine. He looks so weary. "Madi."

I go to him and rest on the other side of the bed.

"You . . . play at Carnegie Hall. You stop at nothing. That was your dream. You do it."

This sounds too much like a goodbye. I already narrowly missed one. No one can expect me to deal with another, not even Dad. I won't negate Dominic's attempt at optimism and refuse to let myself cry.

"You're going to see me play, remember?" I kiss his knuckles. "You'll watch. You will. And you're going to be so proud."

Dad smiles at me as best he can. "I already am."

"Do you want to get up?" Dominic asks. "Watch TV? I think there's a game on."

"No," Dad says, sounding drowsy. "No. I think I'll sleep a little."

Dominic turns back the sheets with my help, but then overwhelmed by the day, by seeing the two most important men in my life reunited, I step back.

I watch as Dominic delicately adjusts my father's position. It occurs to me just how small and frail Dad has become, how difficult it is for him to eat now. He used to be the strongest man in my world, a real live superhero. Now he's thin and gaunt. A sharp mind trapped in a body turned against him.

But even in weariness, he's still my father, my hero in every way. Watching how Dominic works with care and reverence, I'm beginning to believe he's someone else's hero too.

Dominic ensures Dad is comfortable, pulls the covers over his body slowly, and tucks him in.

"You saved my life today, James," he says softly to Dad, smiling at him. "That's not something I think I'll ever be able to repay."

Dad is sleepy. "Nothing to . . . repay. It's what you do . . . for family."

Dominic gazes at him before glancing at me. Being speechless never seems to last long, and he smiles back at Dad, appreciative.

"Yeah? Well, I guess you're right, Pops. I'll remember that."

Dad chuckles weakly. "You know . . . I always wanted a son," he admits, tearing up and sniffling. "I always . . . "

Dominic wraps his arms around him and holds him. I slip away to dry my own eyes, giving them their moment.

When I go back to check on them, Dad's asleep.

Dominic leaves the door slightly ajar, then joins me in the hallway.

"We'll let him rest. He needs it, after all this stress."

But it isn't rest Dad needed. It was Dominic.

He checks on Dad throughout the night. The doctor doesn't even get a chance to make a house call the following afternoon.

At dawn, when Dominic goes to fetch him while I make his breakfast, he's already gone.

I will never forget the sound of grief that erupted from his room, the closest thing to an anguished cry I have ever heard anyone utter, deep, loud, and mechanical, like grating metal, but as real and as palpable as my own.

▭

Two weeks later

We buried my father next to my mother. The disturbed earth is still fresh and covered with wreaths and bouquets of flowers.

I visit whenever I can in between settling all of his affairs. The plaque resting on the damp umber soil reads:

James Daniel Hadley
2004-2069
Father. Soldier. Friend.

The funeral was beautiful, and I never imagined seeing so many of Dad's old wartime brothers-in-arms. I expected four, maybe five, but dozens arrived to pay their respects. He was given a three-volley salute, and Chloe and I were presented with a folded flag. We haven't spoken since, except through Dad's lawyer handling his estate.

It's better that way. Sometimes, blood is just blood. Family is something more.

Dominic wasn't allowed anywhere near the funeral, much to my frustration. I brought him to the viewing to say goodbye, but Chloe's husband made such a fuss that Dominic thought it best he not attend. I couldn't force him. When everyone else left while the casket was lowered into the ground, I stayed. And that was when he showed, to wrap his arms around me and be there.

The house is so quiet. I keep expecting to hear Dad greet me when I move into the lounge or see him sleeping in his bed when I pass his room. The silence is deafening, and I can't handle it. I can't sleep in my bed even though my body is exhausted. My mind never rests.

Instead, I put on one of his old shirts that still smells like his cologne. I curl up with blankets on the couch and watch his favorite Westerns and wrestling reruns, his wheelchair vacant next to me.

Then I cry until I can't keep my eyes open anymore.

Daylight is more manageable. I keep myself busy making arrangements, and Dominic stays in touch daily, busy as well. He's no longer needed as a caregiver, and he hasn't stayed the night since Dad passed away. I imagine being in the house hurts him just as much as it injures me. He said he has things to take care of with Kyrone. We've seen each other a handful of times. Grief-stricken, I wonder if it was always going to be this way, if our mutual love of my dad was all there was to bring us together, and now we'll just naturally drift apart.

I wonder bleakly if he wishes he never met me. Met Dad.

I'm filled with all kinds of regret. That I spent so much time stressing over things like finances and medical care, always moving, instead of slowing down and cherishing those quiet moments when my dad was still here.

Feeling low and unable to concentrate on matters of his estate, I decide to steal away to see Dad. I clean myself up minimally, tying my hair into a bun and dressing in a pair of loose athletic shorts and my dad's worn U.S. Army T-shirt. Fuck makeup.

Fuck everything.

But then, under a drizzling, overcast sky, someone else is there waiting for me as I approach in my 1969 Ford Mustang.

I grasp my umbrella over my head, breath catching in my throat.

"Madi," Dominic says, standing in the rain. The water doesn't seem to bother him.

I go to him, embracing him tightly. "You're all wet. How long have you been waiting?"

"Long enough." He rubs the back of his neck. "Was talking to Pops here."

"Yeah? What was he saying?"

"Oh, the usual. *Get your head out of your ass, soldier. Take care of my baby girl.* That type of thing." He smiles at me. "I miss you, Madi. I've been thinking."

"Yeah?" I smile back. "About what?"

"About what it was like being with you," Dominic says. "I know I haven't been around, and I'm sorry. It's only because I've been getting things in order with Ky."

"What kind of things?"

Dominic takes my hand in his. "Finances. Contracts. The whole shebang."

"You're contracted?" I ask.

His eyes meet mine. "I was. I'm not anymore."

Glancing at my dad's resting place, I slowly turn, walking with Dominic toward the Mustang. His own ride is parked on the other side. I hook my arm around his elbow, gazing up at him as I hold the umbrella over both of our heads.

"I think I'm done competing."

"What?" My eyes widen. "That's—are you serious? But you love fighting."

"I did. Definitely gave me something to do. I'll always enjoy the sport, but . . . " Dominic looks at me. "I think it's time to pack up, put down roots somewhere else."

"Like where?"

"New York. So you can play at Carnegie Hall, just like James talked about. Kyrone knows some Pro-Bionic folks up there who can get me an actual job, working security for some folks."

We stop in front of my car.

"I want to be with you, Madi," he tells me, and his words unleash a veritable army of butterflies in my stomach. "I want to see you play in concert halls. It's *your* time now. And whether that's New York, London, in the back of a pickup truck . . . "

"You can't fit a grand piano in the back of a pickup truck," I manage, trying to refrain from laughing.

"Give me a break. I'm trying to be sensitive here. It's hard work." Dominic pulls me into his arms, and tilts my head up. "I love you, Madison Hadley. People will say I don't, or I can't, or whatever else, but it don't matter. I know I do. Maybe I always have. Wherever you go, I need to be there. I belong with you. Fuckin' A, slap your name in those little registration fields and *own* me for all I care. I'm already yours. I want you to be mine too."

Our kiss is desperate, filled with heat and longing, like we've both been dying of thirst and discovered the oasis we've always been looking for in each other.

When we break away, he teases me. "You really know how to make a man sweat it out."

Part of me wonders if it's all right to be giddy. If the promise of a future in a faraway place should excite me as much as it does, standing here right now in a quiet, country cemetery with the shadow of the Vanderbilt Bridge far away in the distance, holding together a city that always innovates and never sleeps.

But I can hear my father in my head, encouraging me that this is what he would have wanted. That there will still be time for grief and sorrow, alongside healing and hope.

Dominic opens my car door for me. "You really gonna leave me hanging here, princess?"

I lean in to kiss him, and he meets me halfway. "I love you." The words have never felt more right. I pepper his lips with more soft kisses. "I love you. I love you. I do."

He holds me close, resting his forehead against mine. "We're gonna make him proud, Mads," he whispers, white eyes aglow. "You and me."

My heart is so full. I don't know if I believe in an afterlife, but if there was one, this is where Dad would be.

Not in any one place, but with us. Dominic and me. It's an encouraging thought.

"Maybe we already do," I reply, feeling my stomach settle, my muscles relax.

From now on, I'm living like Dad's watching over me. And I'll never quit on myself again.

"Attagirl." He helps me into my seat, taking my

umbrella for me, shaking it out, and shutting it. "Let's get you home."

I beam up hopefully at him. "I'll beat you there."

He strides toward his car with a confident smirk. "Oh, you're on."

EPILOGUE

ONE YEAR LATER

Madison is an absolute hit in New York.

Granted, she isn't like, a pop star kind of hit. It's a different crowd with classical music, but a crowd nonetheless. Her colleagues are kinda snobby for my taste, but overall, they're good people, and they don't even blink when Madison introduces me to them as her boyfriend Dominic Johnson.

Yeah, I took Ky's name for now as kind of a thank-you. So what? I'm sentimental, all right?

It took her a year to get back into the swing of things, which was fine by me. That was an amazing year. Just us and her piano in an apartment that fits our style. Our nights are filled with passion, our mornings with laughter and affection. James's picture is on the mantel, so he can watch his baby girl finally letting go and living her dreams. She brings in cash from performing and teaching these cute little kids from all over the world. Colleges are breathing down her neck, trying to convince her to teach at a university level. She might yet. She hasn't decided. Either way is fine with me.

Me? I'm raking in a decent salary with the security gigs Ky got set up for me. Celebrities, millionaires, politicians, you name it. Occasionally I get to punch some dumbshit's lights out, and nobody makes a big deal out of it. Guess it's different when you're paid to do it.

All these kids she's teaching are giving her baby fever something fierce. She's been leaving adoption pamphlets in the kitchen here and there, and she doesn't have to worry. I definitely get the hint. And I'm all for it. She doesn't know it yet, but I've been ring shopping. I finally picked out the perfect one yesterday.

Just because I'm bionic doesn't mean I don't know how these things work. I've got the proposal all planned out. She's always wanted a dog, and the puppy I'm picking up in a couple of weeks is gonna melt her heart. She won't even see it coming. I plan on making her mine, the way I'm hers. I'm going to love her for her whole life and mine together.

I am Dominic.

Haters can say what they want, but fuck them. I've been alive this whole goddamn time.

AUTHOR'S NOTE

Hey, book bestie! So glad you're here!

I hope you enjoyed the third volume of my debut cyberpunk romance epic, the New Carnegie Androids series.

It'd mean the *world* to me if you could rate and review the book, now that you're finished!

Honest reviews are really the best way you can support an author after reading a book. *I read every single review I get!*

And don't forget, you have the free prequel to the NCA series waiting for you at roxiemcclaine.com! It's a full story you won't want to miss.

Thanks again for reading, and I hope we'll talk soon!
With love, RM

ABOUT THE AUTHOR

Roxie McClaine is a Sci-Fi, Fantasy & Paranormal Romance author. She can be found most days obsessing over Star Wars, superheroes and Supernatural with her equally nerdy husband of four years.

They're current argument is about which Star Trek series is the best. Roxie likes the Original Series. Her husband prefers The Next Generation. But they both agree on one thing, at least: Star Trek is *fucking* awesome.

Follow Roxie on Social Media!

I love receiving reviews! Review Dominic on:

Amazon

GoodReads and Bookbub

Your free book is waiting for you at roxiemcclaine.com

Made in the USA
Columbia, SC
26 July 2022